Praise for

RAY GORDON MYSTERIES

"The humor and suspense elements are so entertaining that I read this in one sitting."

- Idaho Statesman

"I loved the plot, became highly attached to the characters and enjoyed learning a bit about chess all at the same time."

- Long and Short Reviews

"Ray is someone within reach of the average person, chess player or not."   *- Campfire Chess*

"If you are looking for something new and fresh in the crime genre, look no further. I enjoyed this book from page one."

- Carey O., Amazon customer

"Awesome chess and murder mystery!"

- Amazon Customer

"...worth every dinner you miss and every wink of sleep you miss in the process of reading."

- Goodreads review

Other Books by
Michael Weitz

Even Dead Men Play Chess
The Grandmaster's King

www.michael-weitz.com

TILL TOMORROW

MICHAEL WEITZ

Black Fence Books

Till Tomorrow
by Michael Weitz
Copyright © Michael Weitz, 2016

...

...

Published by Black Fence Books, 2016

...

ISBN: 978-0692717783

Published in the United States of America
Editor: JoAnne Soper-Cook

For
Catherine

Always

1

■ The police cruiser was gaining fast. I'd noticed the flashing red and blue strobes in the rear view mirror only a couple of seconds before and already the car was within a hundred yards and closing. Whatever the emergency was this cop was not taking it lightly. I took my foot off the gas, pulled over in front of a row of mailboxes near a side street and looked at Carla. "Must be something serious," I said.

The siren's scream was deafening as the cruiser slowed and came up beside us. Morphy howled in harmony either to join the siren in song or to drown it out of his sensitive ears. He always howled when sirens were near, even at home, but I never knew why. I looked out the side window just as the cop braked hard. The cruiser's tires locked up, skidded across the pavement and sent up a plume of bluish white smoke. Then the cop cranked the wheel to the right, stomped on the gas again and sped up the road I'd stopped just short of.

"That's why you don't turn down a street to get out of the way," I said.

"Thanks, MacGruff," Carla said. "I'll be sure to tell my mom and dad." She winked.

Straight ahead another police cruiser sped toward us. Its headlights flashed left and right along with the red and blue strobes rippling across the top. Its sirens wailed a different tune than the big boxy ambulance I'd just spied coming up from behind and slowing to make the turn in front of us. The ambulance didn't skid into a Hollywood turn, but rumbled around us with as much speed as it safely could. It blocked our view of the oncoming police cruiser for only a moment, but once it passed, the patrol car was right in front of us and didn't appear to be slowing down.

The police officer's eyes widened as if our presence on the side of the road was a surprise. He frantically spun the steering wheel and hit the brakes, which locked up the rear wheels and trailed smoke much like his predecessor did, but it was too late. The rear end of the police car drifted around and towards us, the eerily still tires bouncing and skidding over the black pavement.

"Hold on!" I yelled. I pulled the shifter into reverse and stomped the gas pedal. The gravel spit out from the spinning tires, we shot backward and Carla covered her face with her hands. The back end of the squad car slid toward us, missed by what felt like a millimeter and smashed through the mailboxes. I braked hard and we lurched in our seats.

Morphy yelped and Carla breathed hard and said, "Wow!"

"You okay?" I asked.

She nodded. "That was close."

I twisted to see Morphy lying down and panting. He looked at me like he wanted to know if I'd ever learn how to drive. "Could have been worse, pal," I said and rubbed his head.

The police car backed up a foot, dislodged itself from the wrecked mailboxes and then sped off down the road, its rear passenger door and back fender covered in small dents and scratches. "You sure you're okay?" I asked Carla.

She nodded. "Yeah, I'm fine."

I got out of the car and looked at the damage, which, thankfully, wasn't much. Four mailboxes had been mounted to a wooden rail and pieces lay scattered like a bomb had gone off. The passenger side headlamp of the Land Cruiser was shattered, probably by mailbox shrapnel. I photographed the skid marks on the road as well as the ruts in the gravel shoulder from the Land Cruiser. I took a couple of wide shots from different angles and then hopped back into the car. "Now, let's go see what this is all about."

I turned the key, told Morphy to lie down, nodded at Carla and steered down the road to the right.

We were on the edge of town so the neighborhood wasn't as populated as those just a block or two closer. Some of the houses were set far back from the street and were enclosed by wide-board fences. We saw horses in the front yards of a couple, orchards in the back yards of others. Homes closer to the street appeared more urban and didn't have any farm animals beyond a dog lying on the front porch, but there was still plenty of open space between neighbors — hundreds of feet is some cases, hundreds of yards in others.

It was at the front of one of the non-farm homes we saw the two police cars and the ambulance parked akimbo outside a white rail fence. The house was a single story ranch style the color of an ancient yellow billiard ball, lusterless and beaten. The lawn was kept nice and there were asters and chrysanthemums in the flowerbeds beneath the front windows. No animals or children's toys in sight, just a home in need of a coat of paint with a stunning view of snow-capped mountains.

I pulled over and crunched to a stop on the gravel shoulder behind the patrol car I was sure would soon be the talk of postal workers and rural mailbox owners statewide. We got out and Carla leaned against the fender of the Land Cruiser while I took a few pictures of the police car with my smart phone.

"Hey! What are you doing?" a man shouted. I turned and saw a blue-uniformed cop striding across the lawn. "Sir? Yes, you," he said. "What are you doing?" He kept walking as he spoke and paused only long enough to tall step his way over the fence. In another five steps he was in front of me with his hands on his hips. He was shorter than me by a couple of inches but was in better shape. His graying brown hair was shorn into a crew cut and he wore a dark blue turtleneck beneath his uniform shirt. I guessed to the locals it wasn't jacket weather yet. "Well?" he said.

"Taking pictures of the damage, sir," I said and motioned to the squad car. "Your other responding officer almost slid into me up at the turn off, but took out a row of mailboxes. I need a new headlight though."

His eyes widened when he looked at the damage and then his face relaxed in what looked like a mask of exasperation and resignation. "You were the one who pulled over right before the turn?" he asked. I nodded. "Not the best place to stop," he said. I shrugged. There was no point arguing with the man. "Okay," he sighed, "go into town and file a report at City Hall. We're kind of busy here and it's going to be a long night."

"Who should I tell them sent me?" I asked. His brow wrinkled and he looked from me to Carla and back again. "We're from out of town," I said. "I just thought…" but before I could finish, I was interrupted by a retching sound that would make a Hollywood Foley artist snap to attention. The officer I was speaking with turned around while Carla and I craned our necks to see who was sick.

One of the EMTs from the ambulance was on all fours, vomiting over the side of the front porch. "That's not good," Carla said. Then the young officer, whose car had destroyed the mailbox stand, came out onto the porch and leaned over the medic. "You okay?" we heard him say. Then the medic arched his back like a cat and vomited again, this time emitting more of a gurgly cough. The young officer stood quickly, as if to get out of the way, walked to the other side of the porch, hovered momentarily like he was admiring the clouds on the horizon, and then leaned over the rail and puked all over a clematis bush.

"Oh hell," the cop in front of me muttered. "Pitt," he said. "I'm Lieutenant Pitt. I need to go." He trotted back to the house without another word or glance back at us.

"Wow," Carla said and stepped next to me. "What do you think is in there?"

I shook my head. "Probably a body that's been in there for a week or more. I imagine the smell would make them sick like that. Maybe a suicide. A shotgun blast to the head would…"

"Thanks for that image," Carla said.

"Wasn't a shotgun."

Carla and I turned to the source of the voice, a boy of about fourteen or fifteen wearing a gray knit cap on his head with a fringe of black hair trying to escape. He wore a black t-shirt emblazoned with a yellow Batman logo, baggy jeans with fashionable, factory-made holes and gray skater shoes. "It was worse," he said.

"How do you know that?" I asked.

"I found him." His face turned the color of kindergarten paste at the memory but he quickly regained his composure. "I threw up too," he said with a nod to the men on the porch.

"What happened?" Carla asked.

The boy pulled his phone from a deep pocket, pushed here and there on the screen and handed it over. I took it and held it horizontally so Carla could see as well. After the second picture though, she turned away. As I swiped through the photos on the phone, it was abundantly clear the person inside the house had died recently and did not die by his own hand. The victim was slashed multiple times, the wounds gaping and ragged, blood spatter all over the walls.

It was like he'd been torn apart.

"What's your name, son?" I asked. It struck me as odd that I'd called him son. Why did that term pop into the vocabulary of any adult talking to a young man in times of need? No one said, "What's your name, daughter?" to a young girl under the same circumstances. Weird.

"Gabe Anderson," he said.

"Hi. I'm Ray Gordon, this is my girlfriend Carla." I shook his hand and gave him his phone back. "How did you happen to find the body?"

"I always come by here after school. I live up there another few miles. Dan's door was open but he wasn't outside so I went to see if he was home and shut it for him if he wasn't."

"Did you already talk to the police?"

He nodded. "A little. We're waiting for my mom to show up and then we'll talk more."

"You okay?" I asked. He shrugged. "What do you think happened here?"

"Gabe!" Lt. Pitt called. "I see your mom coming. Come on down here, son."

Gabe put his phone in his pocket and started to walk toward Lt. Pitt. He stopped and stood still a moment. He looked back and his face was ashen. "It was a werewolf," he said.

2

■ We arrived at the Cedar Lake Lodge later than we'd anticipated, but bloody crime scenes tended to slow the world down and make mundane things like hotel reservations seem a little less important. The lodge was a 1920s-era resort planted at the western shore of the long lake and surrounded by pristine forest, quiet mountains and air so fresh, big-city people thought they were breathing pure oxygen. The lobby was dominated by a massive river rock fireplace opposite the check-in counter and had a crackling fire going. I suspected there was always a fire going to add charm. The space in front of the fire was filled with comfortable chairs and couches, each with a table nearby which was stacked with books. No TVs, radios or other noisy electronic distractions. A few trophy mounts were scattered about the walls: four deer, a coyote, a bobcat, three fish and a moose head the size of a car. If it weren't for the modern clothes on the guests I might have thought we'd somehow slipped into the golden age of zoot suits, fedoras and big band music.

The opening round of the chess tournament I'd come to play in was scheduled for the next morning and not surprisingly, there were plenty of people in the lobby playing chess. At big tournaments there were often vendors selling boards, chess sets, books and whatever kind of knick-knacks a company could make chess related, like corkscrews, t-shirts, USB drives and backpacks. The Cedar Lake Chess Tournament was more of a local affair though and the only thing resembling a vendor was a man charging five dollars for a game of speed chess. He had a worn vinyl roll-up board and grimy pieces along with a hand-written cardboard placard that read: *$5/game. You 3mins, Me 2mins.*

"What does that mean?" Carla asked and pointed at the sign.

"It's speed chess," I said. "For five bucks you get three minutes on your clock and he gets two."

"To play the whole game?"

I nodded. "It's a different style of play. All tactics, no strategy. Well, the strategy is for the opponent to cave to time pressure."

"Are you going to give it a shot?"

"Nope, not right now anyway. If he's hanging a sign at a tournament full of chess players he must be good. I played a guy in New York once, in Washington Square. He beat me pretty quickly. It's fun, but a different mindset than traditional time controls."

I spied Perry Whitton and his gray, 1950s-style pompadour, talking to a couple near the front desk and steered Carla over to him. Perry was the organizer of the chess tournament and something of a big wig on the Jasper City Council (so I gathered). We'd met years earlier at the National Open in Las Vegas. When he told me about his idea for the tournament, he'd dubbed it a "chess-cation," a weeklong chess event with one round played per day—since a game might take three to four hours— and that would allow for some relaxation and chess-centric contemplation in the beautiful forests of Oregon. When he learned I was from Seattle he cajoled me into promising I would play in it. I'd made that promise three years before. Now, since Carla and I were making the most of acquainting ourselves as lovers after having spent a lifetime as friends, Cedar Lake Lodge seemed like a fine idea. It just so happened (purely by coincidence I tried to tell her) that a chess tournament was also being held the same week so while I concerned myself with the royal game, she would be able to get in some reading and exploring. She hadn't bought the coincidence part, but there we were.

"Ray," Perry said with a smile and shook my hand, "you finally made it."

"Hi, Perry. I'm looking forward to a great tournament." It had been over a year since I'd seen Perry at a tournament in Portland, Oregon. He hadn't changed much physically, but his demeanor was already more relaxed than I remembered. He was no longer the salesman. I was there to play in the Cedar Lake Tournament. The sale was final.

"I think it will be a memorable one for you." He looked at Carla and beamed like a movie star from the golden age of Hollywood. "Who do we have here?"

"Perry Whitton, this is Carla Caplicki."

They shook hands and Carla said, "Nice to meet you. Ray has told me a lot about you. I'm glad we could make it this time."

"Me too," Perry said and patted her hand. "I'm glad you *both* made it. Have you checked in yet?"

I shook my head. "Just walked in."

He turned back to the counter and waved over the couple he'd been talking with when I saw him. The man was about 6'4" and a fit 220lbs or so; the woman, who I assumed was his wife, looked to be 5'7" and had the shoulders of someone who swam in the lake all summer. They were dressed neatly in dark jeans and button-down shirts and while he had a bit of gray in his black hair, hers was a rich blonde and coifed just at her shoulders. "Jake, Wendy," Perry said, "this is Ray Gordon and Carla Caplicki. They're here for the chess tournament and personal friends of mine. They need to check in."

"Everyone is a personal friend of yours, Perry," Jake said and smiled.

"Those are the only kind to have." Perry looked at us. "Am I right?"

I patted him on the shoulder. "Absolutely."

He nodded. "Ray, Carla, this is Jake and Wendy Humboldt. They are the proprietors of Cedar Lake Lodge and have lived in Jasper forever, just like me. This lodge is a wonderful asset to the town. You're going to love your stay."

"It's very nice to meet the both of you," Wendy said.

Jake pulled an old-fashioned ledger from further down the counter and said, "You're a bit later than we expected, Gordon, but we didn't give away your room."

"You mean cabin. I specifically booked cabin number six." Staying in a cabin was the only way I was able to bring Morphy. If we got bumped to a room in the lodge I'd have to find some doggy motel for my pal and it would take a lot of treats before he'd forgive me.

"Yes, we have you down for number six. The views of the lake are stunning, right?"

He must have written the brochure because it's exactly what it said, but I didn't rent cabin number six for its stunning views.

"Why *are* you late, Ray?" Perry asked. "Was your drive down okay?"

I looked at Carla and wondered if she too felt like we were being grilled. Since when did hoteliers concern themselves with arrival times? She shrugged but I didn't know if she agreed with my thoughts or was waiting for me to answer Perry's question. "The drive down was fine," I said. "We came across a crime scene just outside of town though and got a little sidetracked."

"Crime scene?" Jake said. "What are you talking about?"

"Just north of town, not too far out. I don't remember the name of the road, but—"

"What happened?" Wendy asked. "Why do you say it was a crime scene?"

"A man was killed inside his house."

"Killed?" Perry asked. "What, like *murdered*?"

Carla and I both nodded. "Looks that way," I said.

"Did you hear a name?" Jake asked.

"The kid who found the body said his name was Dan."

Jake's face went white. "Christ," he said. "I need to call Bill."

He turned, went through a door and we all looked at Wendy. Her eyes welled up with tears and she looked at Perry. "There's only one Dan north of town."

Perry nodded, reached across the counter and gripped her hand.

3

■ The trip to Cedar Lake Lodge had Carla and I in the car for hours and it was topped off by a gruesome murder scene. We'd both slept soundly regardless of Morphy's long-snouted trombone snoring and I woke the next morning ready for a battle over the board.

I hugged my shoulders as I walked the fifty yards to the lodge and then warmed myself in the lobby by staring down the soulless glass eyes of the taxidermied game animals. Part of me, maybe an instinctual part, understood the trophies. They were more than mere woodland decoration, they were trophies, the physical manifestation of bragging rights. And the bigger they were...

"Gordon, right?" a voice behind me asked. I nodded and turned from the massive moose head jutting from the wall and faced Jake Humboldt. "Hey, I'm sorry about yesterday. The guy who was killed was an old friend Wendy and I grew up with. Kind of a shock, you know?"

I nodded again. "Sorry. If I'd known, I would have been a bit gentler with the news. I'm not used to small towns where everyone knows everyone."

Jake put his hands in his pockets and looked at the moose. "Pretty impressive, isn't he?"

"He's a big one, alright."

"Everybody who comes in here is amazed; don't matter who they are, right? His name's Otto." Jake's voice lowered to almost a whisper and he said the name *Otto* with reverence, like he was summoning a ghost.

"Otto the moose?" I said. "Otto? Seriously?" Not only did they stuff the head and cantilever it to a wall, they named it too. I suddenly envisioned the moose head strapped to the grill of a truck and making its way down Main Street as part of the locale high school's homecoming parade.

Jake nodded. "He's named after the guy who found him."

"Found him? Otto wasn't a hunter?" What kind of person walks around in search of gigantic dead animals?

"Oh yeah, he was a hunter alright," he said as if I should know everyone in Oregon is a hunter—or at least they should be, "but the moose was already dead." Now Jake was smiling.

"Okay," I said, "I'll bite. What's the story?"

The lodge owner bounced his eyebrows at me and cocked his head toward a pair of well-worn leather chairs near the fireplace. We sat down and leaned toward each other conspiratorially over the table. "The thing about Otto," Jake whispered, "is that he wasn't just a dead moose, right? His body was ripped to shreds."

It was the second time in as many days I'd been met with a body described as being torn up. Was that a

Jasper phenomenon for the dead? I wasn't sure why Jake kept ending his sentences with *right?* or why he was whispering, but I guessed this was a tale he told often and the low voice was for dramatic effect. "You see the scars?" Jake said and nodded toward the moose head. I looked and saw the four ragged, fur-less lines that raked their way from just below Otto's right eye, over the bulbous snout and then disappeared at the lip line. I had attributed them to poor handling during a move, but it sounded like Jake was going to tell me otherwise. "Well those were just scratches compared to the rest of him. The carcass was torn open, blood everywhere, even up higher on the trees. One of his legs was a few feet away from the rest of the body and the guts were everywhere. Otto puked just from the sight of it."

"What did it?" I asked. "A cougar?"

Jake shook his head. "That's the strange part. A cougar wouldn't do that kind of damage, right? Otto said it looked like a grenade went off in the moose's belly and it just exploded bits and pieces all over."

I frowned and my nose crinkled at the thought of a moose bomb. "Had to be a cougar," I said.

Jake smiled. "Maybe. Thing is, moose are big and they're mean. They may look dumb and docile, but they're not scared of anything, right? Don't let the old cartoons fool you." He shook his head and stared out the window. "No, I don't think it was a cougar."

"What do you think it was then?"

"I don't know, Gordon. I was pretty young when Otto was found. People have their theories though. Lots of theories." He patted my knee in a grandfatherly way, stood up and walked back to the front desk. "Lots of theories," he said again.

The first round of the annual Cedar Lake Chess tournament was about to get started and I was concerned how I would play with images of moose viscera splattered throughout the woods on my mind. The tournament was more of a regional event. It was sanctioned by the United States Chess Federation, but because it was more than an hour drive from any major city, only people who really wanted to play made the trip into the wilds of Oregon.

I looked up my pairing on the notice board and found my table. I sat behind the black pieces I was assigned and adjusted them so they stood in the center of the squares and the knights faced the King and Queen rather than across the board. My opponent was Ryan Brooks, who was also known within the chess community as "Smudge" because of the snack food residue he tended to leave on anything he touched — including, and most annoyingly — chess pieces. He was the only person playing in the tourney that I recognized. No one else was a regular in the Seattle chess scene or any of the national matches I'd been involved in.

Smudge arrived about five minutes before the round was to begin. He'd gained some weight since I'd last seen him. He reminded me of the seals I sometimes saw lazing on the wharves around Puget Sound, but he wasn't in hippo territory. Yet. He dropped into his chair at terminal velocity and rattled the table. While I readjusted my pieces, he tore open a family size bag of Cheetos and placed it to the side of the board. Then he unscrewed the cap of a 2-liter plastic bottle of some blue carbonated drink, but I missed the name as he set it on the floor.

With his preparations finished, he turned his attention to me. I nodded. "How've you been Ryan?"

Nothing. Not a sound, not even a blink. He stared at me coldly, as if I'd insulted his lineage.

When I saw his name on the list, I wondered what our meeting would be like. A few months before I'd essentially accused him of murder during the US Chess Championship and the Seattle police had hauled him in for questioning and generally made him very uncomfortable. Even though Smudge was innocent, I was right about him being in the room with the victim so I didn't feel too bad about it. He was sitting on information that eventually helped solve the case.

"Nice place for a chess tournament, huh?" I tried. Still nothing, but his stare was steady. "Fine," I said, "if that's the way you want it." I stared back, a flat, almost bored expression. We either looked like two prizefighters in the center of the ring, or two fourth graders locked in a game of Who Blinks First.

When the tournament director said, "Start your clocks," I reached out, slapped the plunger to start Ryan's clock—and he punched me.

4

■ Getting decked by your opponent isn't something chess players normally have to worry about. I hit the floor on my back and rubbed my jaw. I stared at Ryan, wondering if he was going to attack again, but Perry Whitton popped into my field of view and yelled, "What is going on here?"

"Don't worry about it, Perry," I said. The blow stunned me and I glanced at the other players to gauge their level of curiosity in what I should do. My muscles tensed as I stood up and I took a step toward Smudge but Perry put his hands on my chest and pushed me back. *Keep cool, Ray. Keep cool. Think it through.* Why had a guy I hadn't seen in months suddenly attack me? Okay, I had accused him of murder and the police ruined his day because of it. But in all fairness, the US Chess Championship had been cancelled so he didn't have a shot anyway. "It's okay," I said. "I'm not going to press charges or anything. Let's just play." I picked up my chair and made to sit down.

"No way," Perry said. "I will not have brawling at my tournament." He stopped our game clock and picked up our score sheets. "Ray Gordon wins by forfeit. Mr. Brooks, you may play the remaining rounds, but consider yourself warned."

Smudge grabbed up his snacks and left the room with a smile on his face, but it looked more like evil satisfaction than the joy of victory. I shook my head and wondered if he'd even thought about playing chess when he'd seen our pairing or if blunt force trauma was all he had in mind.

The tournament was being played in what was essentially the basement of Cedar Lake Lodge, but it was well lit, had an old hand-carved bar that was open on the weekends and was quiet even when other guests were around on the main floor. I went upstairs and eyed Otto the moose on my way out the back door.

It was after lunchtime and the sun was already on its downward arc. The back deck of Cedar Lake Lodge ran the length of the building and overlooked a lush green lawn and an army of trees that spread down to a rocky beach along the water. It was like an immaculate green shag carpet punctured by hundred-year-old pine trees that stood as straight as pencils and provided a vertical city for the society of squirrels that raced around the property. I looked out over the still blue lake and took a deep breath before descending the stairs and crossing the lawn to our private cabin.

Cedar Lake Lodge consisted of the main building, a rustic three-story lodge—four if you counted the basement—with twenty rooms, the lobby area, and the dining room; but there were also ten cabins scattered among the trees. When Carla and I booked the trip we insisted on one of the cabins because even though Cedar

Lake Lodge had a strict no pet policy, I wasn't about to leave Morphy at home or in the care of some canine boarding house. Morphy isn't just my dog, he's my pal, my confidant and go-to guy. He goes where I go—unless I fly. Morphy hasn't liked planes since the first time I took him to a tournament in Arizona. Airline regulations required that Morphy, being a dog, had to be put in a pet crate and stowed like baggage in the belly of the plane. When we landed and I was able to see him again, he was trembling, his ears were flattened and the door to his cage was coated with vomit. He spent most of the week in the air-conditioned hotel room with only occasional walks among the desert hills. When the tournament was over I rented a car and we drove back to Seattle.

I unlocked the cabin door and went inside. The layout was a simple set of squares, two rooms bookending a small bathroom in the middle. To the right of the front door was the living room furnished with a couch and loveseat, both of which were upholstered with a western theme of dark green trees and soaring brown eagles. Hideous and unworthy of any home, but somehow it fit. A thin table of honey-colored pine stooped awkwardly between the couches and an end table of the same construction was in the corner. A stone fireplace against the right wall dominated the living room. A small door in the corner, tall enough for a garden gnome, opened up to a covered stoop piled with firewood.

The kitchenette was just inside the front door and the counter wrapped around to the bathroom. To the left was the bedroom with a king size mattress covered, amazingly, by a bedspread of the same design as the couch, and a small wardrobe. A dresser was placed beneath the window and two tree stumps (de-barked, sanded and finished) sat in the corners and acted as nightstands, each with a lamp at the ready. The bathroom was also accessible from the bedroom so in essence, I could walk a circle through the cabin.

Morphy pushed himself up from in front of the fireplace and plodded over to greet me, his tail wagging furiously. I rubbed his head and gently pulled his ears. "Hey, buddy," I said.

Carla was stretched out on the sofa with a book. She was wearing tight jeans, wool socks and a faded purple sweatshirt with the word HUSKIES struggling to remain on the chest through one more spin cycle. Her hair was the color of hot toffee and flowed thick around her shoulders when she stood up. "That was fast," she said.

"Who said chess was slow?" I put my hands on her hips and pulled her close. "You need a new sweatshirt," I said.

"What do you have in mind?"

"I don't know. I should probably get a better look at this one so I can get an idea of what you like, but it would be easier to inspect if you weren't wearing it." She smiled and I maneuvered my hands under the material so my palms were against her warm, smooth skin at the small of her back. I slid them up over her ribs, pushing the bottom of the sweatshirt up.

Carla raised her arms to let me pull it over her head, but then her face scrunched up as if she'd just heard an outburst of bodily sounds from the next aisle over at the grocery store. She took a step back and her sweatshirt, faded logo and all, fell back down to cover her curves. "What happened to your face?" she asked.

My shoulders slumped and I sighed. A combination of facial concern and a question beginning with, "What happened to…" was a guaranteed demise of sexual activity no matter how far along it had come.

"Rough game of chess," I said.

"You're kidding."

"Nope. I'm ready to play and who sits down on the other side of the board? Ryan Brooks of all people."

"Who?"

"Smudge."

"Come again?"

Having been so close to disheveling the hideous bedspread, the joke here was just too easy. But I let it go since Carla was in full-on information intake mode and humor, especially man-humor of the "wink-wink" variety, was of no interest to her. Instead I reminded her how the evidence we found at the scene of Charlie Roggenbuck's death during the US Chess Championship in Seattle had led me to send the police after Ryan Brooks, AKA Smudge, and question him for murder. I had been right that Smudge was there, but he wasn't the killer. Apparently he still held a grudge.

"And he just hit you?" Carla asked. "Did he say anything?"

I shook my head. "Nope. I think he was going to play, though, because he got all of his snacks prepared. Then, *pow*! Game over. I won though, by forfeit."

"At least you can put a positive spin on it," she said.

I took a step toward her. "Speaking of which, how about I take you for a spin?"

She smiled demurely. "Well, I suppose there is something sexy about a couple of brawling chess players."

I put my hands on her hips and pulled her close but before our lips met there was a knock at the cabin door. "You have got to be kidding me," I grumbled. "Who is it? And it better be important."

"It's Wendy Humboldt, the lodge owner. I just need a quick word."

Carla and I both looked at Morphy. Dogs weren't allowed.

"Stall her," Carla whispered and grabbed Morphy.

"Uh, just a second Wendy. We're, uh...not decent," I called.

Carla shot a look over her shoulder that told me we'd discuss my choice of stalling tactics as she pushed Morphy out the little firewood door. She held her palm up in front of his face in a "halt" gesture and closed the door. I tossed his doggy bed to the bedroom and untucked my shirt as Carla plucked the dog biscuits off the counter on her way into the bedroom.

I pulled the door open and breathed out. "Hi. Sorry. Is there a problem?" I asked.

Wendy was frowning slightly, perhaps from having been made to wait, but her sense of customer service took over and her shapely eyebrows realigned themselves into a worried tent.

"Ah, Mr. Gordon. I heard there was a fight, or rather, an altercation this morning at the chess tournament, and..." Her gaze drifted over my shoulder and I turned to see Carla emerge from the bedroom. Her hair was a shambles, like ravaged cotton candy and she was tugging her sweatshirt down—backwards.

"What's going on?" Carla asked.

I turned back to Wendy with a bemused smile. "Oh, I'm so sorry," she stammered, "I didn't realize..." I was surprised to see her face was the color of a rubber kickball. She did operate a hotel after all.

"Yeah," I said, "you were saying something about this morning."

"Exactly. Uh, I just wanted to make sure everything was…well…" She cleared her throat and snuck a quick look at Carla.

I nodded, took a step back and held the screen door open for her. "Alright?" I asked, finishing her thought. "Yes, I'm fine, thanks. Would you like to come in?" I asked.

Carla moved in front of the couch, arched her back in her best stripperesque stretch and eased onto the cushions just as Wendy stepped inside. "Sorry," she said again. Carla smiled.

She looked around the floor and nodded. "Well, it looks like you're fine. There is a first aid kit in the bathroom if you need it. I'm sorry to have bothered you two."

"It's no problem," I said opening the door for her. "There's a guy in the tournament who doesn't like me much, that's all."

Wendy nodded, stepped over the threshold and gave me a short wave.

As soon as I shut the door, Carla jumped up and pulled open the firewood door. Morphy ducked down to look inside and thumped his tail against the sawn logs. "Good boy, Morph," I said and patted my thigh. "Come on!" Morphy lowered his head and hindquarters and scooted back into the cabin.

"You are mean," I said to Carla as she latched the firewood door and stood up. "Not to Morphy, that was brilliant, but to Wendy. 'What's going on?'" I mimicked with a falsetto voice. "Did you see her face? She looked like a ten-year-old who just walked in on the babysitter and her boyfriend!"

Carla smiled sheepishly and shrugged. "I know. I hated to do it, but it got her out of here didn't it?"

"Yes it did. Now then…"

She scrunched up her face. "I don't think so," she said. "Sorry, but I kind of lost it. You know?"

Crap. "Okay. Well we should probably get out of here for a while before Smudge figures out another reason to get the management in here. How about we head into town?"

"Sounds good."

5

■ The town of Jasper, Oregon is on the opposite end of Cedar Lake and is small enough to contain only one high school. Like many small American towns though, it has an overabundance of banks and bars. Jasper had begun as a logging community and thrived to the thrum of eighteen-wheelers hauling felled trees to the mill and trains pulling sawn planks out to cities all over the U.S. But as the old growth timber was cut down, bare spots spread on the hills and mountains like male pattern baldness and the Jasper locals were no longer surrounded by thick evergreens and dreamy forests. County commissioners were complained to, city council meetings were convened, state recommendations were made and soon the semis were gone, the train tracks were pulled up, the loggers left and the lumber mill rusted out to look like the set of an apocalyptic sci-fi film.

Jasper was rededicated as a vacation hot spot with

a crystal clear lake, rejuvenated forests and crisp mountain air. The abandoned railroad bed was paved over to create a recreational path for walkers, runners, cyclists and other non-motorized activities and the abandoned mill was torn down and sold as scrap. Artists arrived to commune with nature, tasteful hotels and charming bed and breakfasts popped up along with bookstores, bicycle shops and outdoor gear rental outlets. A few taverns held their ground but they'd morphed into restaurants that happened to serve drinks or specialty bars that only served martinis—martinis being a well-known distinction of class. Just ask James Bond.

Carla and I took advantage of the fall sunshine and walked down one side of the four commercial blocks that were Jasper's downtown district. We wanted to bring Morphy but having been punched at the first round of the chess tournament, word got around and hotel guests were sneaking curious looks at me. I imagined Smudge was under the same scrutiny, and the close call with Wendy Humboldt had cemented the feeling. Carla and I couldn't get Morphy out of the cabin unseen.

As we walked hand in hand we noticed other businesses further down the street or a block or two behind Main Street, but the four-block area we wandered was meant for us, the tourists. The stores had quaint, hand-painted wooden signs and the street signs welcomed us to *Historic Downtown Jasper* in a flowery script unlike the blocky green and white signs posted elsewhere. The light poles looked like gas lamps from the Victorian era and were hung with baskets overflowing with colorful explosions of seasonal flowers. The Jasper town council had done well. At least for the tourists. I wondered if the locals enjoyed the frills too, or now that they had a murderer on the loose, was the charming facade just a slap in the face?

Not unexpectedly, especially in a small community, the Dan Tilley murder was the talk of the town. As we walked from store to store, we overheard conversations between the shopkeepers and their employees, couples on the street talked with other couples and it was all about the bloody death of one of their own.

We stopped into the Java Pit for a latte and to rest our feet. A man and a woman wearing casual business clothes (my guess was real estate or insurance agents) were gabbing over their foamy coffee drinks. "I just spoke with him a few days ago," the woman said. Her blond hair was pulled into a fashionable ponytail and her designer glasses flashed when she turned her head.

"Where at?" the man asked. He looked to be in his forties, just a touch of gray frosting his temples and he wore soft leather shoes that probably cost more than the rest of his outfit combined.

"At the store," she replied. "I wonder how everyone there is holding up."

The man sipped his coffee. "They'll be okay eventually. Do you think it's true though? The rumors, I mean."

When the woman didn't reply I refocused and saw them both looking at me. *Busted.* I smiled and said, "Nice weather, huh?" I should have asked what the rumors were.

The man frowned and the woman rolled her eyes. They hunched closer over their small table and notched their conversation down to whispers. I looked at Carla and shrugged.

After window-shopping a little more Carla and I detoured into the Juggernaut—*did all of Jasper's businesses begin with the letter J?*—a bookstore with a sandwich board on the sidewalk advertising an author signing going on. Carla pulled my elbow. "Come on, let's go in and see what the book's about."

"My guess is something to do with either cowboys or trees. Or maybe, I don't know, ping-pong." It was the first thing that popped into my head that wasn't chess. No idea why.

"Ping-pong?"

I shrugged. "You never know."

"Okay, you're on. My guess is the book isn't about any of those three."

We pushed through the door and stopped dead. The store was stuffed with people. Many customers were standing together in clusters talking in low tones, the listeners wide-eyed and nodding. Every person not standing in the meet-the-author line had a newly purchased copy of the same book, presumably the one being signed by the author somewhere in the back, but I couldn't glimpse the title. Carla and I took our places at the end of the line and looked around. The two women we stood behind turned when they felt our presence and smiled the way one might at a funeral when seeing someone you don't know. It was an *I understand* smile.

"Hi," I said to them. "Big day at the book store, huh?" I smiled.

One of them nodded and they turned back around.

"Do you notice anything odd about these people?" I asked Carla.

She casually looked around and shook her head. "No. What?"

"Look how old they are. They all know each other too. I think we're the only tourists here."

"Maybe. They aren't talking about ping-pong either. Do you want to change your bet?"

I shook my head but I could tell I wasn't going to win. "Whatever the book is about though," I said, "it's more serious than evergreens." There was an underlying murmur among the groups I couldn't quite make out, but their knowing, conspiratorial looks suggested a long-held secret was being whispered about.

The line moved forward at a steady pace and after rounding a shelf of cookbooks (*1001 Recipes for Lentils!*) I saw a table situated in the center of a small clearing with more bookshelves beyond. Seated at the table was a man thin enough to model for stick figure drawings, except his head was shaped like an artichoke rather than a circle. His hair was the color of rainclouds and flopped over his collar as if he was too busy to manage a cut and style. He wore a thin black leather jacket of the city dweller variety rather than the motorcycle ilk, but it hung like a bell over his thin frame. His old-fashioned Van Dyke beard was sharply trimmed in contrast with his rumpled hair and his deep brown eyes held each approaching customer with suspicious curiosity.

An easel stood to the right side of the table and displayed a poster of the book cover. A neon green star taped to the corner read, "Meet the author!" I read the title of the book and said, "You have got to be kidding."

"What's the matter?" Carla asked.

I nodded toward the poster. "*Werewolves of the Western United States* by Dr. Franklin Thuringer. Doctor of what?"

"Anthropology would be my guess," Carla whispered.

"Veterinarian would be mine," I said.

"Either way, you lost the bet," she said with a smile.

I shook my head. "No I didn't. If this book is about werewolves, then trees play a major part."

"How do you figure that?"

"Werewolves live in forests, or, at least while they're werewolfing. Every wolfman movie features at least one forest scene."

Carla shook her head. "*An American Werewolf in London* takes place in the city."

"Impressive, Miss Caplicki, but he was bitten on the moors."

"There aren't any trees on the moors. That's why they're moors."

"Hmm, true enough, but he *dreams* of being in a forest," I said triumphantly, and maybe a bit too loudly. A few people looked in our direction, frowning like I was an unruly child. "I still win!" I whispered.

Carla rolled her eyes as the line moved forward and we found ourselves at the author's table. I slid one of his books off the stack next to him and looked it over. The cover was dark green with the silhouette of a stalking werewolf at the bottom and a full moon in the corner. The title was a basic font across the middle. I flipped it over and looked at the black and white photo of the man who was currently seated at the table. Same clothes, same aura of superiority. "Have there been a lot of werewolf sightings in the U.S., Dr. Thuringer?" I asked. "I thought werewolves were more of a British affliction."

"It's 'Turing-ger,'" he said. "The h is silent with a hard g. *Tur-ing-ger*. To answer your question, no, there haven't been many cases of lycanthropy reported in the United States. Obviously, however, there have been enough instances to write a book about." He smiled thinly.

"Okay," I said drawing it out. I slid the thin volume back onto the top of the stack. "Didn't mean to offend."

Thuringer looked down his thin nose as I replaced the book. He sniffed once as if his academic prose was far above my reading comprehension level anyway. "None taken," he said. "Few people pronounce my name correctly the first time."

Carla pulled the book I'd put back off the stack and thrust it at him. "I'm sure it's fascinating, Doctor," she said. "Will you sign it? To Carla and Ray." I rolled my eyes.

"I take it neither of you are from here?" he said as he took some time to sign the book and then handed it back. He pronounced neither as *nigh*-ther.

"No, we're not," Carla said. "How did you know?"

"Because this town is where the most famous alleged werewolf killing in the U.S. took place." He tapped the book in Carla's hands. "Chapter Two," he said.

6

■ *Werewolves of the Western United States* by Dr. Franklin Thuringer—silent h with a hard g—began with a dry introduction of lycanthropy. It outlined the mythology and psychology of the disease in a rather mundane scholarly fashion. Carla told me all of this when she finished the prologue after lunch. I wasn't interested in reading the professor's attempt to add funding to whatever program he was involved in. I was convinced the book was nothing more than embellished stories from drunken campers and was filled with reports of wolfmen tearing through the vineyards of Napa Valley and staging fist fights with the sasquatch (or was that *sasquatches*?) of the northwest. Carla mused that my disinterest was because Thuringer slammed me about his name. Maybe she was right...

Chapter One of Thuringer's book dealt with California sightings and Carla only skimmed it. She dove right into Chapter Two though, and chewed the ends of her hair through the first few pages. "Ray, you need to read this," she said.

I wasn't too keen on reading it. An academic—although that was yet to be determined in Thuringer's case—writing a book about mythical monsters as actual dangers struck me as desperate and perhaps even decidedly *non*-academic. But it did seem to be holding Carla's attention. "It's not about pretty high school students is it?" I asked.

She shook her head. "I wouldn't say that, but something happened to a high school student right here in Jasper. Remember what that boy said out at the scene yesterday? It's got to make you wonder."

"Wonder what?"

"That's why you need to read it."

I read it.

Thuringer's premise was one based on psychology, that lycanthropy was in the mind of the afflicted and not a physical manifestation. The victim only thought they became a werewolf and acted accordingly, like a rabid killer dog. Okay, my opinion of the author went up a few steps.

And then it fell back into the basement when I read,

However, the human mind does not always believe what it sees and will strive for a logical explanation, even if it means creating a fictitious truth. Similarly, seemingly extraordinary things, events or sightings of "mythological" creatures, force the brain to believe it is playing tricks on itself. This may contribute to what we label as sightings when they are, in fact, all too real. And can, albeit rarely, lead to dangerous circumstances that may involve injury or death as believed to be the case in Jasper.

The narration was followed by a muddy photocopy of a local newspaper article dated 1971.

Local boys discover body of girl, 15

JASPER, OR - The ravaged body of Cindy Bickerman, 15, of Jasper, was found Sunday morning by two local boys in a secluded area of the township. Miss Bickerman had been reported missing from her home the day before.

The remains were discovered as the boys played in the wooded area. Town police were called in and aided at the scene by members of the Union County volunteer fire department and several local residents familiar with the area.

Though a wallet was found, official identification of the body found in the woods was necessarily made by means of dental examination. A medical examiner estimated the girl had died sometime on Saturday, October 21st.

Authorities refuse to make any official comparisons to the mutilated corpse of the large bull moose found by local hunter Otto Reinhart last year. However, given the proximity of the two scenes and the damage done to the bodies, it is the opinion of at least two officers who spoke under condition of anonymity that the cases appear to be similar in nature. It was also not lost on those same officers, nor others on the scene, that the moose and the unfortunate young girl were killed under the full moon.

Police are continuing their investigation of the case.

The copy of the article didn't include a byline, which was too bad. It would have been nice to talk to the reporter if he or she were still alive. As gruesome and horrifying as it must have been, Cindy Bickerman's murder had to have been the town's most memorable event since electric lights were installed. What I found interesting was the reporter made a point to mention that Otto the moose and Cindy Bickerman were both killed and similarly mutilated when the moon was full. Pretty sensationalistic for Seventies journalism, I thought. Apparently when the werewolf story about Otto the moose's killer was brought about it was thought to be a joke. But after the discovery of Bickerman's mangled body, people swallowed the idea like honey-coated medicine. Partly because of the similar nature of the injuries and partly because no one wanted to believe any normal person—even someone willing to kill a fifteen-year-old girl—would be capable of such unthinkable mutilation.

Like the newspaper article, Thuringer touched on the most obvious counter theory, that a mountain lion was responsible for the deaths. But forest rangers and biologists at the time agreed it was unlikely. Mountain lions didn't demolish their prey like a toddler throwing food from a high chair. The idea of a rabid predator was tossed around but the only evidence was the ravished corpses of a moose and a teenage girl killed years apart.

The citizens of Jasper believed they had a werewolf on their hands.

At least a majority of them believed it. I didn't think the entire population was in fear of full moons; there had to be a few eye rollers. Given how the bookstore was packed, the way customers stood in protective groups and spoke in frightened undertones, some of them still did though.

The raking claw marks across the moose's snout in the lodge was the only physical evidence left, but the photos in Thuringer's book, taken at the scene of Otto's demise, showed the shredded hide and two limbs torn from the body. Entrails snaked out from the belly like gory tree roots and blood was splashed across the surrounding tree trunks to puddle among the leaves on the ground.

I was glad the photos were black and white.

There weren't any photos of Cindy Bickerman's crime scene in the book. I imagined her parents had a say in that decision, or they were unavailable because of her age. Either way I was happy not to see them. Thuringer quoted several people though, one of whom had been the Jasper Chief of Police and who had witnessed both scenes and attested to the similarity of sheer destruction to the bodies. Other than that, he refused to speculate about the killings being carried out by the same person, persons or creature.

I finished the chapter about the Jasper werewolf killings and closed the book. "Well?" Carla said.

"Weird. Two similar deaths, both out in the woods, but a year apart. Now another killing just the other day, decades later, but not as…messy. According to rumors anyway."

"I know, creepy."

"True, but why only three in such a long span?"

"You want more mutilated bodies?"

"If we're talking about a werewolf, then yes. Full moons aren't rare."

Carla shrugged. "Maybe he moved, but came back. Maybe he found a cure but relapsed. Who knows?"

I wasn't sure if Carla was serious or just toying with me. "Yeah, I believe the only cure is a silver bullet," I said, "but okay, let's say he moved. Let's also assume that as a werewolf he continued to kill over the years. I don't recall any news reports over the years about horribly and mysteriously mutilated bodies. And that's the kind of stuff reporters live for."

"Maybe he was overseas."

"Are you seriously thinking there's a werewolf out there? I mean, I have a pretty open mind, but this," I said tapping the book, "I'm not so sure about."

"Well werewolf or not," Carla said, "something unexplainably violent happened here. Twice with the moose. Maybe three times if that's what happened to that man when we came into town."

I enjoyed the movies. I tolerated (for the most part) academic books like Dr. Franklin Thuringer's, but in the end it was all fiction. I shook my head. "No, whatever happened is definitely explainable. It just hasn't been explained yet."

7

A month before, when I'd called Perry to enter the chess tournament, he had given Carla and me a standing dinner invitation for any or every night we were in Jasper. After a murder in town that had the rumor mill spinning like a meat grinder and the introduction—at least to me—of a werewolf legend, I thought it was the perfect evening to take Perry up on his graciousness, even if it was the first day of the tournament. Nobody else I knew would be able to fill me in on what had happened in this town, and what was happening, better than he could.

Perry's house was on the north side of the lake. It was a summer cabin in his grandfather's day, but as the town grew, it was remodeled and passed down as the family home. After sneaking Morphy out for a quick walk and then getting him settled in the cabin, Carla and I rented a boat from the lodge (very romantic) and cut our way across the water. The lake was smooth and black in the deepening twilight and the trees crowded the shoreline as if they were waiting for something to happen. I shook my head and focused on Carla's lithe form in front of me as she aimed a spotlight to guide our way. She swung the light to the left and we spotted Perry's private dock where his 1933 Chris Craft was moored. I killed the motor a bit too early and we paddled the last thirty yards, drifted up to the opposite side of the pier as Perry's boat, and tied off.

The cabin hadn't been hard to recognize. Perry told me it was the best-lit house on the lake. No other description. It hadn't been noticeable from the lodge as it was hidden by trees, but as we'd drawn closer there was no mistaking it. The dock had four lamps lighting the way to land and then the steps were lit as they zigzagged up the slope like San Francisco's famous Lombard Street. At the top, the interior lights of Perry's home shone out over the lake through windows that allowed an unencumbered view. But the lights weren't harsh, they didn't glare like advertising billboards or make me squint; they were warm and beckoned us to shore and up the stairs like friends.

Perry stood on the deck overlooking the lake. He wore an orange cardigan that would have blended nicely with some 1970s shag carpeting, and held a drink between his palms. The scene reminded me of an ad for over-priced cologne except the clothes wouldn't be orange and Perry would be forty years younger. Other than that, yeah, a cologne ad.

Carla and I climbed the wooden stairs, made the turns and stopped twice to gaze out at the lake. Nearer the top, I could see the grin on Perry's face. "I guess you don't need a gym membership when you've got a set of stairs to climb every day, huh?" I called.

He lifted his glass in a mock salute. "You don't need any help do you?" I waved him off and Carla and I mounted the remaining steps without aid.

"Where's your wife tonight, Perry?" Carla asked. "Ray thought she'd be here."

"Della wanted to be," Perry said, "but she is now on her way to Sacramento at this very moment. Drove to Boise to catch a plane. She got a phone call about lunch time that a friend of hers is pretty sick."

"Oh, I'm sorry to hear that," Carla said.

"Well, at our age we tend to go to more funerals than weddings." He shrugged. "Not to sound morbid or indifferent, it's just the way it is."

Over dinner we talked chess—though not about the current tournament—and Perry tried to embarrass me good-naturedly by bringing up my past. "The last tournament I saw Ray at, I tried to get him to commit to coming here, to play at Cedar Lake," he said, leaning towards Carla, "but all he did was talk about you." Her eyebrows crinkled and she glanced at me. "Oh, you weren't an item yet," Perry went on, seeing her confusion, "but it bothered him you see, even if he wouldn't say it, that you were seeing someone else. It doesn't matter though, does it? Ray once again said he would try to come to my tournament, and the two of you are together now." He raised his glass of wine and said, "Here's to good friends, better friends" (with a wink to Carla) "and of course, to chess." We clinked our glasses and drank to his toast while Carla smiled to herself and I kicked Perry under the table. "And speaking of chess," Perry continued, "what was that all about this morning? Why did Ryan Brooks take a swing at you?"

I told Perry the story behind Ryan's animosity and he nodded. "I'm not sure why he's still mad though," I admitted.

Perry nodded and took a bite of the trout he'd prepared for dinner. "He's got a chip on his shoulder I imagine. He doesn't know how to deal with his frustrations, which is probably why he eats the way he does and you're an easy outlet."

"Wow, when did you become a psychoanalyst?" I said.

"Or maybe he just holds his grudges and he's not through with you yet. I'd be upset too if you accused me of murder." He winked at Carla and took another bite.

"Okay, Perry," I said, "I'll try not to accuse you of anything. But, since you sort of brought it up, I would like to talk about the so-called werewolf killings."

"Oh, that reminds me, there's something I want to show you, see what you think. Come into the living room."

"I'll clear these plates up," Carla offered as we all stood.

"I'll help," I said.

"No, you go into the living room."

"Uh uh. I think you should be part of this discussion too, 'Miss-Believes-in-Werewolves.'"

"I didn't say I believe in werewolves."

"You want to though." I smiled.

We all cleared the dining table and stacked the dishes in the kitchen sink. "Coffee while we're in here?" Perry said.

"I'd love some, thank you," Carla said. I nodded and Perry took three mugs from a cabinet and set about creating the brew.

When we were seated in the living room, Perry in an over-stuffed leather recliner and Carla and I knocking knees in a matching loveseat, he said, "You obviously have something on your mind, Ray. How about you go first."

"Okay. Well, Carla and I picked up that book this afternoon, the one the author was signing at the little book store downtown."

Perry nodded. "I've read it."

He didn't smile when he admitted to knowing the work in question. I frowned. "And? What's your take on the 'Jasper Werewolf'? You were here when that big moose and the girl were killed weren't you? Are you going to tell me that you believe they were brutally murdered a year or so apart by a werewolf and that same creature struck again the other day?" Perry took a sip of his coffee and stared through me like he was in a daze. "Well?"

"There's no werewolf," he said. "Of course there's not."

I looked at Carla, not as an I-told-you-so, but more in relief. "What's the real story then?" I asked, turning back to Perry. "Or at least the official theory."

"I'm going to need something stronger than coffee for this conversation," he said. "Either of you want a nip?" Carla and I both shook our heads and stayed on the loveseat.

While Perry poured himself a stiff one in the kitchen I looked around the main room of the house. Like the exterior, the inside was more home than cabin. Oiled mahogany panels covered the lower third of the walls while the upper sections were painted a rich maroon the color of aging rose petals. Large paintings depicted snow-capped mountains, rivers, and warmly lit homes nestled in deep valleys, but the centerpiece was the fireplace built of round river stones not unlike those of the fireplace at the lodge.

Perry came back in, negotiated another log onto the fire and then sat down. He gently held a snifter in his palm and swirled the copper liquor. He sipped the drink and took a deep breath. "Now then," he said, "you're staying at the lodge so I know Jake must have told you some sort of story about Otto."

I nodded.

"Who's Otto?" Carla asked.

"He's the moose head hanging on the wall at the lodge," I said.

"Right," Perry confirmed. "First thought to have been savagely killed by a rabid or otherwise deranged cougar and later lumped into the local werewolf myth."

"And you know all of the facts?" I asked.

"Most of them. Some of the truth has yet to be revealed though."

"Otto wasn't killed by a cougar was he?" I asked, though it wasn't really a question.

"Nope."

"And you know this for sure how?"

Perry held my gaze for a moment. "I know who shot him," he finally said.

"Shot him?" I said. "What was he shot with, a grenade launcher?"

Perry took another sip of his brandy and settled back into the embrace of his chair. "It's more than likely that sometime in his life Otto had a disagreement with a cougar—that's where the scars on his nose came from—but it's not how he died. He was shot by one of the locals who was far beyond three sheets to the wind. Said it was an accident of course."

"An accident? How do you accidentally shoot a moose that big?"

"Scared the shit out of him is what he said. Pardon my French, Carla. Apparently he was sitting against a tree finishing up a bottle of bourbon and was planning on doing some target practice…"

"Excuse me," said Carla. "He purposely got drunk before firing a high-powered rifle?"

Perry shrugged. "I said he was a local. I didn't say he was a PhD. Anyway, he chucks the bottle out as far as he can, but it hits a rock and shatters. Right then he hears a grunt or a snort or something from the brush next to him and then this giant creature just stands right up!" Perry chuckled a little and took another sip of his drink. "So the anti-hero of the story starts screaming and shoots three or four times. He thought it was Bigfoot or something! Scared the crap out of him! He's out there long enough to finish off a bottle of booze and the whole time the biggest moose in the Pacific Northwest is napping right next to him."

"How do you know this?" I asked.

"Because I saw his underpants! He literally got the…"

"Perry, I get that he was scared. How do you know all of the details?"

He sighed. "He was a friend of mine and I was one of four others who helped cover it up."

Carla's eyes bulged and the itchiness on my chin was the carpet when my jaw hit the floor. "Covered it up?" I said. "You? Why?"

"Like I said, he was a friend. He was going through a rough time: no job, his girlfriend had left him, just a bad time for him. He was already on probation for driving without a license or something and we didn't want him to get arrested for poaching so we…hid the evidence. It probably would have been fine if we'd just told the truth but we had been drinking and we got scared."

"I saw the pictures, Perry. What did you do?"

"Okay, I'm going to tell you, but please remember, there's a lot of wisdom between now and then. We were young, we were drinking and back then it seemed like a good idea. And it was kind of funny. At least it was then. It's not now." He took a deep breath and said, "We blew up the moose."

8

■ Carla and I didn't talk much on the way back to the lodge. As the boat slowly putt-putted across the dark lake, I suspect both of our thoughts were kneading the story of Otto the moose.

Not only was Perry part of the cover-up, but so was Jasper's current Chief of Police, a prominent furniture store owner, and two other men who had moved away after college. In a brilliant flash of lager-induced ingenuity, the group of friends decided the best way to hide the evidence of an accidentally poached bull moose was to blow it up. One of the four friends was able to procure a quarter-stick of dynamite—from another friend who "knew someone"—and pushed it into one of the bullet holes in the chest of the beast. Together, with the help of a lighter tied to a long branch, they lit the fuse and ran like hell.

When they went back to see how their plan had worked, each and every one of them threw up, one started crying and they swore to never tell anyone what they'd done. And it worked, too. Rumors, theories and stories were invented around how the moose had been obliterated but no one ever discovered the truth—until Cindy Bickerman was found torn to pieces in the woods a few years later.

Bill Blunt was a young officer when Cindy's body was found and a near-panic engulfed the town once the story of her demise went public. He made up his mind to tell his chief about his earlier role in Otto's explosive end. Eventually the chief learned the whole story and who was involved, but by then it was too late, the rumors had been fortified, the legend forged and the favorite, with Cindy's morbid death so close to Halloween, was the Jasper Werewolf. The townspeople collectively decided it was better to live with a myth than with the knowledge that one of their own could commit such a vicious, unthinkably savage act.

Bill's chief, without having to figure out how Otto's death figured into that of the Bickerman girl, decided to let the werewolf idea perpetuate and hopefully draw the killer out. He'd read how some murderers crave attention and if nobody in Jasper suspected a person but rather a thing, a creature of the night, then maybe the real killer would become frustrated and let it slip to someone what he'd done.

It was a gamble and a poor bet at that, but there was precious little evidence and no leads. The police were stumped, the citizens were scared and the legend of the werewolf grew.

I cut the boat's engine and steered toward the pier while Carla aimed a blinding spotlight to guide me. The boat bumped against a few old tires lining the dock and I tied the lead rope to the mooring pin. I'd never been a boat person, but just knowing the correct terminology made me feel quite nautical. I stepped onto the pier and gave Carla my hand to steady her climb out of the boat.

It was almost 11 pm as we made our way across the expanse of lawn and through the black pine trees toward the lodge. Warm light from within the old building cast stretched squares of yellow into the night and I reached out for Carla's hand. "How about a nightcap in the lobby after I turn in the boat key?" I asked.

"Sounds good to me, but let's not sit where I can see Otto the moose."

"Deal," I agreed and glanced back towards the lodge. That's when a tree moved to its left and into our path. At least it looked like a tree. The lights from the lodge were behind the big man and turned him into a silhouette. Carla's grip tightened around my fingers and then relaxed. "It's Jake," she whispered.

"Did you think we were lost out on the water, Jake?" I said.

"I'm not Jake," said the man in a low voice I didn't recognize. "But you're Ray Gordon, aren't you?"

Carla's grip tightened once more as we moved closer to the stranger. I angled our steps to the right and into a clearer view of the lodge and to also keep myself between him and Carla. "That's me," I said. "And you are?"

The man stopped and turned so the light from the lodge window illuminated half of his face. "I'm Cal Pederson," he said. "The new pairings are up. You and I play in the next round."

"How'd you know who I am?"

"Recognized you from the picture."

"What picture?"

Cal smiled and pointed to my face. "From your fight with Ryan Brooks. Someone got a picture on their phone and put it up by the pairings."

"I wouldn't call a cheap shot a fight," I said. "Nice meeting you, Cal." I pulled Carla into a quick walk and marched up the steps to the lodge, determined to see the picture.

The lobby was peppered with guests, many of them chess players. I recognized a few and gave them each a quick wave. "Why don't you grab us a table while I go check the pairings," I told Carla.

"Didn't you just meet the guy you'll be playing?" she smirked.

"Okay," I admitted, "I'm going to go tear down that picture."

"Can I see it?"

"Depends," I said and headed down to the basement.

When I came back upstairs, I found Carla sitting at a secluded table with her back towards Otto the moose. I slid into the booth next to her and asked if she'd ordered anything yet.

"You weren't gone long enough for the waitress to notice I'd sat down," she said. "So do I get to see the picture of your boxing match?"

"I accidentally tore it to bits," I said with a shrug. "Oops." The picture was of me on the floor with a look of both shock and bewilderment smeared across my face. Whoever the photographer was, it was clear he'd had no formal training and was just another victim of cell phone advertising. The composition was shoddy at best, as the photo was taken from above rather than at eye-level, the image was slightly blurry as either the photographer or I was moving at the time of the exposure and the lighting was tinted green from the fluorescent bulbs in the drop-down ceiling. Basic stuff. Obviously the picture was taken without any forethought and poor snapshots just weren't worthy of such an esteemed event as the Cedar Lake Chess Tournament.

The waitress was a woman in her 40s who looked like she needed a few nights away from the kids, a little tired but enjoying her job. She wore black slacks, a tight white blouse and a short black apron. Her hair was the color of whiskey and pulled into a ponytail held in place by a crimson ribbon.

Each table she stopped at was granted a conversation beyond menu choices. While I watched her take an order from the table next to us something witty was said and the waitress let loose a barrage of laughter that rattled the room like machine gun fire. Carla and I looked at one another and raised our eyebrows — whether in surprise or alarm, I wasn't sure.

When the waitress sidled up to our table I caught an eyeful of her breasts testing the tensile strength of the blouse and then, artfully, notched my gaze up a bit. The plastic tag pinned to her blouse was etched with the name Carey. "You," she said looking at me, "must be here for the chess tournament."

"Yes, but how did you know it's me and not her?" I asked, and tilted my head toward Carla.

"Well, it's true I haven't seen either of you in here before, but your shirt kind of gave you away." She smiled and gave me a wink. "Now, what can I get you two?"

I looked down at my chest while Carla ordered a martini. I was wearing my *Chess Players do it at Knight* t-shirt under the button-up I'd worn to dinner. I'd opened a couple of buttons when we entered the warm lodge.

Carey the Waitress was smiling at me when I looked up at her. "And you, Mr. Chess Player?"

"Double bourbon," I said. It wasn't my regular drink but it sounded tough.

"What did you think of Perry's story?" I asked Carla as Carey wiggled back to the bar.

"It's all I could think of when we came across the lake."

I nodded. "Me too."

"Well, he proved you were right. There's no werewolf and you have an explanation."

"For the moose, yes. I'm sure you noticed though, that he didn't admit to his little group of buddies blowing up Cindy Bickerman."

"Yes, I noticed that. But like you said before, there must be an explanation."

"Sure. And my guess is someone in this town knows what it is. The guy who was killed the other day? It's not a coincidence that his body was in the same condition as that girl."

Carey returned and set our drinks down. "Thank you," Carla and I both said. Carey smiled but we didn't say anything more so she moved to another table for some chitchat.

"What I don't get," Carla said quietly, "is if it's the same killer, why has it been so long between victims? Why now?"

"You want more murders?" I asked and smiled.

"You know what I mean. Usually serial killers...*need* I guess is the word, to kill more often than once every few decades. You know? So why so long?"

I nodded. "How long does it take to research a given topic and write a book about it?"

"Really? Dr. Thuringer?"

I shrugged. "Just throwing it out there. Like you said, *why now?* What's the link between Cindy Bickerman, the guy who was just murdered and what's going on in this town right now?"

Carla shook her head.

"The werewolf," I said.

"Are you saying Dr. Thuringer murders people in order to drum up sales?"

"I've heard of worse motives. The only other thing going on right now is the chess tournament, but it wasn't around in the 1970s and as far as I know, neither Cindy or the other guy were chess players. He wasn't in the tournament anyway. But an author writing about obscure legends might need to create an interest beyond horror movie buffs. Remember how busy that bookstore was when we went in? Just like everyone else in town, they were talking about Jasper's most recent murder. Don't you think it was pretty convenient for the author that a werewolf-style killing took place only a day before his book signing? Just enough time for the gruesome details to make their way around town."

"Ray, that would be horrible if it were true."

I shrugged. "Like I said, just a theory. Besides, I don't know of any…"

Wendy Humboldt's voice broke the convivial atmosphere in the lobby bar like a glass bottle tossed up and allowed to shatter on the floor in the middle of us all. "You did what?" she yelled. Her voice was high, maybe even panicky. Then the office door slammed shut and the customers, including Carla and I, reflexively sipped our drinks and looked around nervously to see if we were the only ones who'd heard something.

Whatever Wendy and Jake were arguing about in their office, the slammed door wasn't a conclusive exclamation mark, nor was it a strong enough barrier to keep us all from hearing it. Their shouting was muffled and pretty difficult to understand where Carla and I sat, but there were one or two people sitting near the office that had developed a slight inclination of their heads towards the voices and seemed only to want a bowl of popcorn to keep them happily eavesdropping on the lodge owners' row.

I wrote our cabin number on the receipt, trapped a five under my empty glass for Carey and stood up. We weren't the only people leaving. The argument spilling out into the bar wasn't business related, it was personal, and the downturned eyes and tight mouths of most of the bar patrons meant Carey's work night was pretty much over. Even so, listening to them, personal or not, was like watching your best friend get spanked by his parents for doing some stunt to impress you. Just not worth hanging around for.

Not everyone was put off, though. As we wound our way through the tables toward the door I made eye contact with a group of three chess players who gawked bleary-eyed at each other with each exclamation that made it through the door. They were drunk, or on the road to drunkenness, and the one in the middle pointed at me, gave me a big smile and raised his glass in a mock salute.

Nearest the office door Kevin Corsmo, the speed chess challenger, sat alone at the bar with his head in his hands as he stared at his untouched drink. It was hard to tell if he was blocking out the argument or listening intently. He didn't move, even when Jake shouted, "I did it for us!" Everyone heard that one, not just those near the office. *Did what?* I thought.

Before Carla and I made it out the door, I spied Carey knocking delicately, almost tentatively on the office door. I presumed she was going to tell the Humboldts their argument was bad for business, not to mention her tips.

9

■ The morning was bright when I woke, but there was a watery feel to the air and clouds were bumping into one another as they made their way through the mountain peaks above the lodge.

A good day for chess.

My game with Cal Pederson was slated for 10 am, which gave me three hours to shower, eat breakfast and go over some tactical puzzles to get ready. I woke Carla and we jumped in the shower together. That led to another kind of togetherness and then I had only two hours for breakfast and prep time. But I wasn't complaining.

We ate breakfast at the lodge and between forkfuls of scrambled eggs and slurps of coffee, Carla flipped through one of my chess books and set up tactical problems on my mini travel set. I took bites of my blueberry muffin and tried to find the checkmate in two moves. It was her way of being involved and I loved her for it.

At 9:45, I went downstairs to the playing room and Carla went to find a spot by the lake to read some more of *Werewolves of the Western United States*. I wasn't thrilled to leave her alone with a killer out there, but it was daylight and whoever was slashing their victims to death B-movie style, they seemed to have a vendetta against citizens of the town, not chess playing tourists or their girlfriends.

Perry Whitton stood by the pairing sheets and compared them to a sheet of paper on his clipboard. Last minute details, I supposed. I raised my chin and asked what board I would be playing on.

He pointed to the back corner with his pen. "Board five," he said. "You're playing black against Cal Pederson."

I smiled and said, "Thanks." Nobody needed to know I had dinner with the tournament director, even if we discussed murder instead of chess. No favorites, simple as that.

At the table I straightened the pieces, turned the Knights to face their King and Queen and placed my score sheet to my right. Everyone has their own quirks. Mine was profiling my Knights, Smudge unpacked his snacks and sometimes punched his opponent, but the strangest habit I'd seen was a player who moved his pieces by grasping each one between his middle and index fingers, like a cigarette. Made it kind of tough in tight time controls when he had to move fast.

I'd never played Cal Pederson before so I didn't know what to expect, but when he sat down in front of me he was one big smile. He didn't adjust his pieces or nudge his score sheet or wear a hat to pull down over his eyes like a TV poker player. He just smiled and said, "I didn't mean to scare you last night. Hope everything was okay."

"No problem," I said. "You just kind of appeared from behind a tree and startled us."

Cal laughed. "I know I'm big, but big as a tree? Come on now." He laughed some more.

"Oh, sorry. I didn't mean to imply…"

He waved me off. "I'm just joshin' with ya. Hey, I see your picture's gone! Did you take it down?"

I shrugged. "Gee, I'm not sure what happened to it."

Cal laughed again.

Perry Whitton cleared his throat then, loudly, as if shushing a classroom full of students. "Quiet down please and we'll get started. As always, if there are any questions, stop your clocks, raise your hand and I will come to you. And please remember to turn in your score sheets; I don't want to track you down somewhere out in the woods. Okay? Start your clocks."

Cal and I shook hands amid the staccato pops of clock plungers being smacked, then I slapped the button on my side and started his clock. He brought his pawn out to d4 and I hunkered down to decide how I wanted to play.

It took almost three hours and forty-three moves, but I was able to maneuver my pieces into a winning position.

BLACK

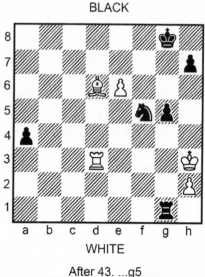

WHITE

After 43. ...g5

After I attacked Cal's Bishop with my Knight, he moved his Rook to d3 to protect it and my plan came into view. My Rook on the g1 square protected the entire g-file and my Knight covered the h4 square; his King was trapped. When he moved his Rook it was too late for him to do anything about the ensnarement and I advanced my pawn to g5. He then brought his Bishop to g3 and in response I brought my h pawn to h5.

Cal looked over the position and shook his head. He reached over, stopped the clocks and shook my hand. There was no way he could stop my pawn coming to g4 and placing his King in checkmate.

"Great game, Ray," he said. "You strangled me there on the side."

"Thanks, Cal. That was a tough one."

I signed my score sheet, gave it to Perry and headed up the stairs.

It was close to half past noon and I was starving. Carla had probably already eaten but I felt like celebrating and walked down to our cabin instead of the lodge dining room. She was on the couch with her feet on the table and Morphy next to her with his head in her lap. When I came in, she lowered the book she was reading—still *Werewolves of the Western United States*—and patted Morphy with her free hand. Morphy thumped his tail against the couch cushion.

"Hey there," Carla said. "Did you win?"

"I did. Tough game though."

"But brilliant, I'm sure. You look tired."

I smiled. "Have you eaten?"

"Not yet, but before you say anything, there's an envelope there for you." She pointed to the small kitchen counter behind me. "It's from Perry. He dropped it off about an hour ago."

"Really? He must have sneaked out of the tournament room…"

"For a bathroom break," Carla finished with a nod. "That's exactly what he said. He wants you to read it first thing if you got back here before 2:00."

I glanced at the clock and tore open the envelope. Perry had written that I could get another point of view about Cindy Bickerman's death from the former medical examiner, Rusty Melman. He ate lunch and had coffee every day at Kathy's Café from noon to 2pm. *Have the waitress point him out*, Perry wrote, *and tell him I told you about Otto's ¼ stick of dynamite.*

I pocketed Perry's note and looked at Carla. "Let's go get some lunch."

10

■ Kathy's Café was a former barbershop and a former ladies' hair salon. Back in Jasper's logging days they were called Fred and Ginger's respectively and had a man and woman, one on each door, reaching toward the other so they appeared to be dancing whenever business was good. Both shops eventually folded and when Kathy bought the building at a discounted price, she tore down the wall in between but kept the long mirrors on the walls and had the barber pole refurbished and hung by the cash register. Booths of forest green vinyl lined the walls and small square tables filled the middle of the room, while old black and white photo enlargements and maps of Jasper's logging heyday gave customers something to look at while they ate.

A sign near the door read, *Seat yourself, we'll see ya!* Carla and I opted for one of the green booths and a teenage waitress brought us menus. "Here for the chess tournament, huh?" she said looking at me.

I looked at Carla then back to the waitress. "How did you know that?"

She shrugged. "How are you doing?"

"Winning, so far. Thanks."

She smiled. "I'll give you a couple of minutes to look things over." She turned and walked away before I could ask her about Rusty Melman.

I turned to Carla. "How, exactly, does a chess player look?"

"Very sexy," she said. "And like you." She laughed.

"Ouch. Just for that you're buying lunch."

We scanned the menu and when our waitress returned, we ordered cheeseburgers and salads. I never eat French fries during a tournament because they weigh me down rather than help me think; it's amazing how different foods affect the brain, not just the waistline. "Can you tell me if Rusty Melman, the former Medical Examiner, is here?" I asked before she had the chance to disappear again.

"Yeah," she said and pointed. "That's him in the back booth."

"Thanks."

I got up and walked the length of the diner to where Rusty sat with a steaming cup of coffee and a novel. Even though he was sitting I could tell he was a tall man since he had to bend slightly in order to rest his elbows on the table. He had wavy white hair that had a shine to it, like new nylon rope, and a full mustache with old-fashioned pointy ends that capped his mouth like a rooftop. He looked thin but not sickly and his hands were sharply defined, the knuckles angling into the fingers like tools rather than flesh. He wore wire-rimmed glasses and a red and blue plaid flannel shirt that was faded enough to make purple feel right at home.

"Dr. Melman?" I asked when I reached his booth.

"Yes?" he said and lowered his book.

"Hi, my name is Ray Gordon. Perry Whitton told me to let you know that he told me about Otto the moose's quarter stick of dynamite. I was wondering if, when you have some time, I might ask a few questions."

He took off his glasses and extended his hand. As I shook it, I could feel the bones but his grip was strong. "Perry told you, huh? How do you know him?" he asked and motioned for me to take the seat across from him.

"I know him through chess," I said. "I'm sorry, I can't sit right now, my friend and I just ordered lunch." I pointed to Carla and she waved.

Melman looked at his watch. "I'll be here for a bit. Come back over when you're through. What exactly is this about, Mr. Gordon?"

"Ray, please. Curiosity mostly. Maybe I can help Perry dispel the local werewolf myth."

"I'm not so sure he wants to lose it," Melman said. "But yes, we'll talk when you're through."

I went back and sat across from Carla. "We can talk to him when we're done," I said.

"This is so cloak and dagger," she said. "It's like you're meeting a contact in some mysterious diner and he's going to divulge an important clue. We better hurry and eat so we can talk to him before the enemy assassinates him!"

"Maybe he knows they're on to him and that's why he sits in the back and watches the door. Seriously though, he said something kind of strange."

"What?"

"I mentioned that I might be able to help Perry do away with the local werewolf story and he said he didn't think Perry would want it gone."

Our lunch arrived before Carla could say anything and we spent most of the meal contriving a plan to liberate Morphy from the cabin and take him for a walk sometime after dinner.

When we finished I asked our young waitress to put Dr. Melman's coffee on our bill. "He doesn't pay for anything," she said and guffawed only like a teenager can. "This is his place."

I wrinkled my brow and asked, "Then who's Kathy?"

"Kathy was his wife. She died about ten years ago. She opened it up so she'd have something to do because he was working all the time."

"How come this isn't Kathy's Kafe, with a *K*?" Carla asked. "Seems like so many places do that sort of thing."

The girl smiled and said, "That's exactly what Kathy wanted to do, but Dr. Melman was against it. He didn't like misspelling things on purpose just to be cute." She rolled her eyes. "Said people's spelling was bad enough."

My opinion of Dr. Melman went up a notch. I thanked her and Carla and I went down to where Rusty Melman was on the last few pages of the book he was reading. Without looking, he motioned us into the seat opposite him and then held up his index finger so we would remain quiet. He turned a page and we watched as his eyes scanned back and forth, drawing in the written word.

When he finished, Rusty closed the book, set it aside and laid his bookmark on top of it. He then took off his glasses and set those on top of the book as well. I got the sense of a ritual taking place. "Nothing like a good book," he said. "Wouldn't you agree? I suppose I should ask if you're readers first, shouldn't I?"

"Oh yes, we are," Carla said, "and I agree with you wholeheartedly."

"Dr. Melman, this is my friend Carla Caplicki."

They shook hands and he asked, "What do you like to read, Carla?"

"I used to read a lot of mysteries, but I've shifted a bit to general fiction and history."

"Why the change if I may ask?"

"Let's just say I've had enough of the criminal mind for a while—fiction or otherwise."

Melman half smiled and nodded. "Fair enough. I'm afraid, though, that Mr. Gordon here is wanting to discuss a particularly gruesome crime that happened many years ago."

Carla nodded. "I read about it in Dr. Thuringer's werewolf book. And I was part of the discussion with Perry."

Melman nodded again and then looked at me as if it were my turn to go on stage. "Perry told me to tell you. I assume you were the M.E. at the time of Cindy Bickerman's death?" I asked.

"Yes. It was the most disturbing thing I'd ever seen—up to then and since. And that's saying something given the high-speed car wrecks and accidental gun shots we tend to get around here."

"Why is that? Why disturbing?" My heartbeat picked up the pace. Did Melman know something that might have been overlooked for years?

"Because it was obvious she was murdered. The idea of someone doing what they did to her. It's why people choose to keep the werewolf story alive."

"How do you know she was murdered?"

"The wounds were made with a knife, or some other sharp-edged tool. They weren't done by any creature, mythological or real. And before you ask, no, they were not self-inflicted. No one could do that to themselves, and besides, there was only one fatal cut; everything else was post-mortem."

Carla turned white and closed her eyes. She shook her head, denying the image access. I squeezed her knee and kept my hand there hoping it might comfort her if at least a little. "Why do that, do you think?" I asked Melman.

He shrugged. "No telling, really. Maybe to hide evidence, maybe they enjoyed it, maybe they couldn't stop. Who knows?"

"Ever see anything like it since?"

He shook his head. "Something like that comes along and it scares you," he said. "That kind of mutilation takes a certain kind of mind in my opinion, and it scares you because if they can do it once, they can do it again, and usually do. A town this small with a Jack the Ripper-style serial killer? We were terrified."

"Which is why you allowed the werewolf story to stick." Understandable to a degree, I thought, but still crazy. Just look at the way the town was reacting to a murder years later.

Melman nodded and sipped his coffee. "So what's your interest in this?" he asked. "It's more than simple curiosity."

I nodded, looked at Carla and back. "We were at the scene of the murder the other day on the outskirts of town."

"You were at the scene? How do you mean?"

I told him how Carla and I had been driving into town when the police car almost slid into us and how Gabe Anderson showed us the photos he'd taken inside the victim's house. "It's not easy to see pictures like that and just forget about it," I said.

"The boy took pictures?" Melman asked incredulously.

Carla and I nodded in unison. "Kids these days, huh?" I said because I didn't really know what else to say.

Melman took his cell phone from his pocket and dialed. He put it to his ear and said, "This is Rusty. Hey, did you know there are pictures of your crime scene out there? Probably all over the Internet by now." He listened a moment and then said, "I'm talking with someone who saw them." I looked at Carla and then Melman said, "Yeah, I know. Okay." He tapped a button on his phone and pocketed it. "Let's go talk to the police," he said.

11

■ Jasper's police station was housed in City Hall, presumably to save the community money and space, but even then it only occupied a small portion of the brick-faced building.

Dr. Melman led Carla and me around the corner from Kathy's Café and a block east of Main Street. Like most towns and cities across the country, government offices, service facilities and other non-retail businesses were found here, just beyond the eye of tourists, but not so far away that the townsfolk had to go looking for them.

Melman opened the door and waved us through. We bypassed the check-in counter where I'd filed the accident report upon our arrival, and walked down a short hallway to another check-in area. This section was labeled *Jasper Police Department* in large painted letters below the counter. A row of plastic chairs lined the wall and faced the counter like a firing squad, and a bulletin board dominated by a high school football schedule that read *Go Lumberjacks!* hung above them. I thought that was just lazy design since anyone sitting wouldn't be able to peruse the bulletin board. Instead they would have to stand with their back to the officer staffing the counter. It just seemed to miss the point of a waiting room.

"Bill's expecting us," Dr. Melman said to the young cop at the counter. Without slowing down to get permission, Rusty led us past the counter and through a door with a sign glued at eye level: *Authorized Personnel Only. Civilians must be accompanied by a police officer.*

Beyond the door was a large open room that smelled like coffee and peanuts. Four desks, each topped with a computer monitor, filled the floor space along with a number of file cabinets and bookshelves pushed up against the walls. A countertop ran the length of the wall under a bank of windows to our right and was topped with three coffee machines, four two-drawer cabinets, a paper slicer and a cardboard box with a teddy bear peeking out from the top. We walked straight past the desks to the back corner where three doors seemed to argue with each other. One appeared to lead outside, the one in the middle had a clear glass pane and opened into an antiseptic hallway and the third, with a frosted pane of glass, was the only one with a sign: *William Blunt, Chief of Police.* Dr. Melman knocked once and opened the door.

"Hi, Bill," Rusty said. "I brought some people I think you might want to talk to. They're the ones I called you about. They're the ones who told me about the photos."

Chief Blunt rose from his chair when he saw Carla, something I suspected he wouldn't have done if it had just been Dr. Melman and myself. Chivalry lived on in small town America. He wore jeans with his button-up shirt and dark blue sports coat. His face was shaped like an olive and topped with a well-oiled mane of ashen hair slicked back into a 1950s or 60s Elvis-style wave. His eyes were too close to one another and seemed to be precariously balanced on each side of his hooked nose.

Introductions were made, hands were shook and we all sat down around the big desk. "Ray Gordon," the chief mused. "Weren't you in here a day or two ago? You claimed one of my officers damaged your car."

I nodded. "Yes, sir, that was me."

"You're also Perry Whitton's chess buddy from Seattle, right? He told me about those murders you solved during the big chess tournament up there."

I nodded again. "I'm sure Perry made more of it than it really was, but yes, an old friend of mine was one of the victims."

"I'm sorry to hear that. Now, how are you involved with what has happened here?"

I started from when Carla and I had seen the flashing lights of the police car coming up fast behind us and we'd pulled over to let it pass, then related how Gabe Anderson showed us the photos he'd taken of the murder victim, the werewolf book and the conversation with Perry about Otto the moose. "And here we are," I concluded.

"And here we are," Chief Blunt repeated. He looked at Carla and then at Dr. Melman who shrugged in a cat's-out-of-the-bag sort of way. Blunt looked at me again and said, "So what do you think?"

His question caught me off guard. Most police chiefs would be upset I knew as much as I did. Then again, a true community leader left politics and egos at the door and did what was best for the people under their care. "Well," I said slowly, "I think there are two possibilities, neither of which are good. One, you have a murderer living among you who kills only once every few decades, or two, you have someone who used Cindy Bickerman's death as a way to style the murder they committed. Either way, whoever killed the man out in his house the other day knew him *and* is cold-blooded enough to have torn him up like that."

"Dan Tilley," Chief Blunt said. "That was the victim you saw the photos of. Lived here all his life." He glanced at Dr. Melman again and a silent message passed between them. I guessed they both must have known the Tilley man. "I'll give you a third possibility," Blunt said, "a thrill kill."

"A what?" Carla asked.

"A thrill kill," the chief repeated. "It's when someone murders just to feel what it's like to take a life."

He looked at Melman who nodded. "I've heard of those. Often teenagers with psychological issues."

"Right," the chief said. "We're holding Gabe Anderson on suspicion of murder. The pictures on his phone are quite convincing evidence."

12

■ It was only a gut feeling, but I was sure Chief Blunt had the wrong person under arrest for the savage murder of Dan Tilley. I'd spoken with Gabe Anderson for only a minute or two at the crime scene, but he didn't strike me as boastful. Instead he was quiet, almost wanting to be rid of the visions he'd seen inside the house—regardless of the fact he'd taken pictures of the body.

"Is he your only suspect?" I asked.

"Yes," Blunt answered, well...bluntly.

"What about..." I stopped and shook my head. "Never mind."

"Mr. Gordon, if you know something..."

I shook my head again. "I don't know anything. I was just tossing an idea around, but I'd rather not say. The last time I accused the wrong person of something like this it cost me a friendship and earned a right cross." I rubbed my jaw and looked at Carla. "Don't need another Smudge situation," I told her. She shook her head.

Chief Blunt leaned his elbows on the desk and breathed hard. He looked like a bull ready to charge. "Mr. Gordon, I must insist…"

I shook my head and stood up. "I'm sorry, Chief, but I won't say anything right now. Tomorrow."

"This is not your investigation, mister," Blunt said rising out of his chair. "I should arrest you right now for obstruction."

"I'm not trying to keep you from doing your job, Chief." I raised my hands and took a step back. Why was he so pissed all of the sudden? "Like you said, this is your crime scene. But I'm not going to accuse someone of murder just because I don't like him. You can understand that, I'm sure." *Couldn't he?* I asked myself. I wasn't the one being unreasonable. There had to be something else going on here.

I felt Carla behind me as Chief Blunt and I stared at one another. He blinked, waved me out of his office and sat back down. The conversation, if it could be called that, was over. I looked at Melman and he shook his head. Chief Blunt didn't even look up as we backed out of his office.

Outside I took Carla's hand and we walked around the block, back to Main Street. Just beyond Kathy's Café, in front of a frozen yogurt shop, we sat on a bench.

"That didn't go very well," Carla said.

"It could have been more congenial."

Carla's eyebrows popped up. "Congenial? I think Chief Blunt wanted to put you in a cell just to show you he could."

"No argument there," I said and I pulled out my phone. "Tommy?" Carla asked.

I nodded and called up his number. Tommy Ryder was a friend of mine in Seattle who I played friendly games of chess with on a regular basis. He also had a knack for finding stuff out.

"Hey, hey, Ray," he said when he answered the phone. "What's up, man? Why are you calling me on your little love jaunt?" Only Tommy would call a chess-based vacation with Carla a 'love jaunt.' His boundary meter was set very low when it came to male/female relations.

He once asked a pretty woman walking down the street if he could touch her coat, to feel the material. She nodded and while he rubbed the coat between his fingers he asked, "Is this wool?"

"Yes," she'd replied.

"I thought so," he said. "Only *ewe* could be so fine."

The woman rolled her eyes and exclaimed, "Seriously?"

Tommy had smiled widely and asked her out just because she was intelligent enough to get his weak humor. She declined and walked away.

In all fairness though, the vacation wasn't all about chess.

"Hi, Tommy," I said. "I need a little help if you have some time."

"Need some pointers, huh?" He laughed and I thought I heard a knee get slapped.

I'd walked into that one. "I'll ignore that," I said and smiled in spite of myself. "No, I need a background check, just whatever information you can find on someone."

"So let me get this straight, you take Carla on a vacation for some alone time and now you're mixed up in something? What's with you?"

"I don't know. Things just happened. It's her fault too!" I glanced at Carla and she squinted at me.

"Whatever. Okay, give me the vitals."

I recited Dr. Thuringer's name, how to spell and pronounce it, the title of his book, publisher and even a quick description of how he looked. "Okay, I'm on it," Tommy said. "How soon do you need it?"

The great thing about Tommy was he didn't ask questions. He would get me the information I needed and then he'd grill me about it the next time we played chess. Get it done now and talk later. "Soon as you can," I told him.

"Will the world end?"

"Maybe."

"Okay, give me till morning."

"Thanks, Tommy."

We disconnected and I looked at Carla. "I didn't give Smudge the benefit of the doubt when I'd sent the cops after him and look how that turned out. I'd rather see what kind of guy this Thuringer is before I tell Blunt about it. Killing for sales is a thin theory, but I'd pick Thuringer as a killer before that Gabe kid."

Carla nodded. "It kind of felt in there like the police just want this done quickly, like they want to prove they can solve it."

"Maybe. I got the feeling there's some worry over it too. They don't want this happening again. You heard Melman; they were terrified the first time it happened. Can you imagine what they all thought when they saw that crime scene? That's why Blunt got so angry at me. He's scared."

13

■ There was still plenty of sunshine left in the day and Carla and I both thought taking Morphy for a daylight walk would be good for all three of us. We'd already created a plan to get him out of the cabin unseen while we'd eaten lunch and we decided to implement it.

The drive from Jasper to the lodge was about fifteen minutes. I called The Wood Guy and asked if he could meet us at our cabin in about a half hour. We arrived with ten minutes to spare and I parked the Land Cruiser near the front door. We opened the rear hatch, left it open and Carla went inside to pack what we needed while I waited outside.

The Wood Guy was Nick, a local who delivered cut and bundled dry wood in varying amounts. People who lived in the area, like Perry Whitton, bought cords of wood from Nick in order to keep the home fires burning through the winter; people like Carla and me, who rented a lodge cabin for a few days, could buy smaller bundles that might last a romantic night or two.

The six cabins between the main lodge and Cedar Lake were built off to the side, away from the central lawn and at a slant to one another so views of the water wouldn't be completely obscured. Occupants of cabins one through five could still see the other structures when they looked toward the lake, but number six was only about thirty yards from the shore and had just the one set of neighbors, which is why I rented it. The other cabins blocked the view of anyone watching from the lodge and by happy coincidence, the couple who had been staying in cabin five had checked out the day before. There was also a thin game trail that led from the cabin, into the thick cover of pine and oak trees along the lake and then up onto the road where we could cross to a campground. Each night we snuck Morphy out of the cabin like a cold war spy and stumbled along leafy trails better navigated in the daylight hours.

The first hitch in our plan was that cabin five had been occupied while Carla and I had been in town. A bright red Honda with California plates was perched in the bare patch of grass next to the cabin and the curtains were thrown open. Getting Morphy out of our cabin unseen had hinged on our having no neighbors. I could easily keep Nick occupied on the side of our cabin while his truck and trailer blocked our front door, but the cabins were built up a few steps from ground level so anyone looking out the window in cabin five would be able to see Carla and Morphy come outside.

The second hitch was when I saw the lodge owner, Jake Humboldt, fast walking toward me like a tourist guide catching up to a slacker from his group. I glanced over my shoulder and saw Carla close our front door. She'd probably been on her way out to see what was taking so long. Then I looked at cabin five and saw a woman standing at the window looking at me. She had long dark hair and wore a green flannel button up over a pair of jeans. She smiled, waved and then walked away from the window just as Jake came to a stop in front of me. "Gordon," he said, "I really need to hire kid to deliver messages." He shook his head and looked at me like he wanted a tip. I stuffed my hands in my pockets and kept them there. "Nick the Wood Guy called and said he wouldn't be able to make your delivery until later this afternoon, maybe around five or so."

I nodded. Part of the quaintness of Cedar Lake Lodge was that with the surrounding mountain peaks, it was near impossible to receive a cellular signal and the only reliable means of communication with the outside world was a single land-line telephone in the lodge lobby or the US Postal Service. "What happened?" I asked. "Is everything all right?"

"Truck trouble or some such," Jake said. No surprise there. The Wood Guy delivered his product via an old brown pick-up truck that seemed to have lost its luster sometime during the Reagan administration. Flaking sheets of plywood stood on the long rails of the bed and were bolted to spears of wood sunk into the stake pockets. Effectively it gave the truck bed almost three times the hauling capacity by going vertical. The plywood was whitewashed and had THE WOOD GUY stenciled in red paint with a phone number beneath. A bug-eyed beaver that looked to have been drawn collectively by the local kindergarten class was in the rear lower corner with the words, *Firewood delivered to your door!* Another old pick-up bed served as a trailer with the same extended plywood walls. Our plan had been to have Nick pull right in front of our cabin and his tall ugly wood delivery truck would block the view of our door, which would give Carla the cover to get Morphy into the back of the Land Cruiser. Not to be.

"Okay, Jake," I said. "Thanks for letting me know." He grunted and ambled back to the lodge. I looked back at cabin five, saw an empty window, and went to find Carla and Morphy.

"What's going on?" Carla asked when I stepped inside. "What did Jake want?"

"Just letting me know that The Wood Guy can't make it until later."

"Well crapola. I was looking forward to a normal walk in the sunshine. I would have even picked up the poop!"

I chuckled. Carla wasn't squeamish, but she didn't usually jump at the chance to pick up after Morphy; she was serious about getting out of the cabin. "I know," I said. "If Morph was a little dog it wouldn't be a problem."

"Why don't we just back the car up to the door and have him jump in?"

Morphy had come out of the bedroom and leaned against my leg so I would scratch his ears. "It's worth a shot," I said. "We have neighbors again though, so we'll have to keep our eyes open."

Carla peeled back the curtain and looked out. "I saw a woman earlier, but no one else," she said. "Maybe she's alone."

"Either way, let's be careful. We still have a few more nights here. Know what I mean?"

She dropped the curtain and turned around, crossed her arms and smiled. "Oh I know exactly what you mean, mister." She sashayed towards me, draped her arms around my neck and spun me around slowly so she was leaning against the kitchen counter. Then she smoothed her palms down the front of my shirt, pushed her hips toward me and reached behind her. With a jingle she grabbed the car keys off the counter and stood up straight. "I'll bring the car around and back it up to the steps," she said and winked.

"Tease!" I called after her as she went out the door.

I stacked the picnic basket and a couple of blankets by the door and clipped Morphy's leash to his collar. As Carla backed the car closer to the steps, I looked at cabin five, up toward the lodge, and down by the lake, but saw no one.

Carla got out, opened the rear lift gate and lifted the window. She glanced around and gave me the thumbs up.

"Ready to go for a ride, Morph?" I asked. He stood up and wagged his tail. He was always ready for a ride. "Okay, into the car then," I said and opened the door.

But Morphy had other ideas. He bounded down the steps instead of jumping into the car and after a quick sniff and a shuffle of paws, he lifted his leg over a chrysanthemum and peed on it.

I threw Carla a blanket and she held it open as wide as her arms would allow in order to block Morphy from the view of our neighbors. I tossed the picnic basket and remaining blanket into the Land Cruiser and then jumped down and snatched Morphy's leash up before he could further explore the flowerbed in front of the cabin. "Come on, Morph," I coaxed. "Let's go for a ride."

He finished his business, jumped up onto the stairs and then into the back of the car. I closed up the lift gate as Carla shook the blanket again for show, refolded it and tossed it to me.

Carla got behind the wheel and once I was strapped into the passenger seat and told Morphy to lie down, we were off. As we passed the lodge, I saw Smudge looking out the lobby window. He had an ugly smile on his face as he pointed at his own eyes and then to us as we drove by. He'd seen us. He'd seen Morphy and the nasty smile said he was going to rat us out like a third grader.

14

■ We drove about three miles into the wilderness behind Cedar Lake Lodge to a trailhead that promised fantastic vistas from the paths it led to. The hike was good in that we were able to stretch our legs and Morphy enjoyed the scents only he could detect. We spotted a pair of deer, found a seemingly hidden pond and gawked at the autumn colors that painted the landscape better than a Renaissance master. But for all the beauty nature provided my senses, my brain kept thinking about Smudge and what awaited us when we got back to the cabin, and Gabe Anderson, the kid who'd found the torn up body and how I truly believed he was innocent of the murder. But why? Gut feelings mean bunk when it comes to the law.

"What's on your mind?" Carla asked.

I'd stopped on the trail and stood like a post as I stared at a maple tree, whose orange and red leaves made it look like a colorful fire. "Have I been quiet?" I asked and turned to her. She raised an eyebrow and smirked. "Well," I said slowly, "I think we're totally busted with Morphy, but I might have an idea about that, at least for tonight. The other thing is the Anderson kid."

For years I'd volunteered at a youth center in Seattle where I taught kids how to play chess. Some of the kids already knew the game so we'd just play, but we would also talk. I wasn't a counselor or a social worker of any kind, just a guy peddling chess (the best brain exercise game ever!) and letting my young opponents get things off their chests if they wanted to. I liked to think I helped, but playing chess with Gabe Anderson wasn't going to get him out of jail or beat a murder charge.

"Maybe Tommy can help," Carla said. "What teenager isn't on the Internet? Tommy can probably find out anything about him you need to know."

I nodded. I'd already asked Tommy to look into Thuringer's background, what was one more? If anything, Gabe Anderson would probably be easier to check out. Even though teenagers seemed superior in their technological savvy, when it came to their personal lives online, it was as if nothing was off-limits and the more information they could put out there for anyone to find, the better. Security, secrecy and any sense of self-preservation were the last things on their mind when they could get hundreds of "likes" for a selfie. Carla was right, if the local police weren't going to dig into Gabe's past to look for a motive and either prove him guilty or innocent, then Tommy could.

I took my cell phone from my pocket but there was no service. "I'll have to call when we get back to town," I said. "Don't let me forget, okay?"

"I won't," Carla smiled.

We'd been on our hike for about an hour and it had culminated at a pristine mountain lake that mirrored the surrounding pine trees and slopes of wildflowers so clearly it looked like the entrance into another dimension, another world with the same lake, trees, flowers, and deep blue sky waiting for us to cross over. I wondered if such a dimension would have inhabitants as brutal and murderous as those we had on earth.

When we returned to our cabin it was almost dark and after a couple hours of hiking Carla and I were in full-on dinner mode. During the drive back we'd mentally gone over the menu at the lodge and made ourselves hungrier by talking about the entrees we had yet to try and what kind of cocktail we'd each begin our evening with.

But it wasn't meant to be.

Before we even came to a stop in the small turn out that served as a parking spot for our cabin, Jake Humboldt and Ryan "Smudge" Brooks were only steps away from the rear of the Land Cruiser. Ryan must have been sitting at the window in his room with a pair of binoculars waiting to pounce. Carla and I got out and walked around to the back of the car to meet them. "Hi, Jake," I said. "Can I do something for you?" I chose to ignore Smudge, acted like he wasn't even there since I knew what was about to happen had been brought about by him. I even turned my shoulder a little in front of him so he couldn't mistake he was being snubbed. It was a little immature, but Smudge moved slightly to get a look at my face and I forced myself not to smile in victory, little as it was.

"Well," Jake started. He shifted his weight like he was about to throw a punch. "Mr. Brooks claims he saw a dog come out from your cabin this afternoon."

"Hasn't it already been established that Smudge—sorry, *Mr. Brooks*—has it in for me?" I asked and rubbed my jaw to help Jake remember why his wife had come to visit me the first day of the tournament.

Carla crossed her arms and leaned against the car as if backing up my ploy. "I think Perry should have disqualified him from the tournament," she said.

Instead of agreeing with that line of thinking and walking back to the lodge though, Jake produced a flashlight from his pocket and clicked it on. "Right. Do you mind if we take a look in your car?" he asked.

"Do you have a warrant?" I countered.

"See?" Ryan said. "If he didn't have his mutt in there he wouldn't care if you looked."

"Can we rummage around your room when we're done, Ryan?" I said. "I can only guess the kinds of reading material we'll find. I bet it's not all chess magazines."

Ryan crossed his arms and scowled but didn't say anything more. I stared at him a moment longer and out of the corner of my eye I saw Carla stick her tongue out at him.

"I'm just kidding, Jake," I said. I unlatched and lifted the back gate of the Land Cruiser and stepped aside so he could inspect the inside. Jake held his flashlight up and swiveled the beam around the empty seats.

Ryan stepped forward. "I saw the dog!" he said.

But there was no dog. Morphy wasn't in the backseat, nor was his blanket, his leash, or any of his toys.

"Wait a minute," Ryan said. "Over here, in the flower bed. There will be tracks. I saw it come over here and pee on the flowers."

I looked at Carla and her eyes were wide. We hadn't thought about Morphy's paw prints in the dirt.

Jake followed Ryan to the flowerbed next to the stairs of our cabin and shone the flashlight beam back and forth across the ground. "I don't understand it," Ryan said. "I *saw* the dog. I swear. Right here!"

Jake snapped off his flashlight and shook his head. "I'm sorry about this, Gordon. You too, miss. If you choose to have dinner at the lodge this evening—and I understand if you don't, right?" he said with a glare aimed at Ryan Brooks, "I'll let them know it's on the house." He took Ryan by the elbow as if he were a disobedient teenager rather than a hotel guest, and steered him back the way they came.

Carla and I watched them for a minute before we looked down at the flowerbed for ourselves. It was dark, but we looked anyway. "I know he stepped right here," I said and pointed at the chrysanthemum plant.

Carla nodded. "We dodged a bullet that's for sure, but I don't know what happened. Squirrels?"

"Nope," I said and pointed over her shoulder. The light had come on inside cabin five and as Carla turned to look, our new neighbor, who was looking out the window at us, picked up a small broom, pointed to it and gave us a thumbs up.

"Huh," Carla said "What do you think about that?"

"I think she has a dog or a cat in there," I said. We waved and mouthed the words *thank you* and then went inside our cabin.

"We need to get her a bottle of wine or something," said Carla.

15

■ Debbie Mathews was from Sacramento, California and was enjoying a fishing vacation on her own while her husband was travelling through Arizona and New Mexico on his motorcycle. They planned to circle around and meet in Las Vegas after another week or two. She'd brought along her small dog, Sydney, a Corgi mix the same golden color as Morphy and with one floppy ear. And lucky for Carla and me, she ended up in cabin five.

After we'd showered and dressed we stopped and knocked on her door to invite her to dinner with us up at the lodge. She said she'd already eaten but asked us inside to meet her dog since we were all breaking the same rule. "It's tough to leave them sometimes," Debbie said and motioned at Sydney. "I just don't have the heart to leave her behind in a kennel."

I smiled. "No need to explain. Morphy goes everywhere with us." Carla looked at me with a smile and after a moment I realized it was because I had said *us* and not *me*.

"How long are you staying here?" Carla asked Debbie.

"Depends on the Kokanee."

"I'm sorry? The what?" I asked.

"The Kokanee. They're why I'm here. Cedar Lake is legendary for Kokanee. A few years ago a twenty-three pounder was caught out in the middle of the lake. The guy was trolling about sixty feet down with flashers. I'll start at sixty but I don't have any flashers, might try some wedding rings though. Close enough, right?" She smiled.

Carla and I looked at each other like we were in a foreign land and didn't speak the language. "What's a Kokanee?" Carla asked Debbie.

Our new neighbor's smile fell. "It's a salmon."

"Oh." Carla nodded.

"There's trout, too," Debbie went on. "No need to troll for those though, just cast from the shore. Basic worms and eggs for them. Sydney doesn't always like to go trolling. Plus I have to keep her out of sight anyway."

"I didn't see a boat," I said.

Debbie shook her head. "They rent them here. I didn't feel like driving the truck and hauling the boat all the way up here. This way if the fish aren't biting I can pick up and head to the next lake."

Carla and I nodded as if we understood what Debbie was talking about. As far as I knew the Pacific Northwest was famous for Chinook salmon. I'd never heard of a Kokanee and the only flashers and wedding rings I knew about belonged in jail and on fingers.

Debbie picked up on Carla's and my lack of fishing knowledge and changed the subject. She said, "I didn't know there was a chess tournament going on though. Did you?" At least she didn't automatically assume I was in it. Not that I was embarrassed to be a chess player, but I found it rather odd how complete strangers kept identifying me as one of the entrants.

"Yes," Carla said, "that's actually why we're here. Ray is going to win it."

"Uh oh," Debbie said with a smile, "pressure's on now."

As Carla and I walked to the lodge I thought about what Debbie had told us about Ryan Brooks. She didn't know his name of course, but she knew Jake from when she'd checked in. After Carla and I had left for our hike, Debbie watched as Smudge walked down to our cabin and tried to look in the windows. It was his looking at the flower bed that got Debbie's attention and after he'd gone back to the lodge she went over, saw Morphy's paw prints and decided to sweep them away. She said Ryan just looked like he was up to no good and we had looked like nicer people.

I smiled at that but was surprised by Smudge's determination. Was he really bear-hugging a grudge or was it something more? During the US Chess Championship I'd asked the police to question him because I had a suspicion he had at the very least been playing chess with someone who was shortly thereafter murdered in cold blood. The Championship had eventually been cancelled without any victor so his being questioned by the police had no overriding outcome on his being able to win. Ryan was smart enough to realize that. Maybe it had affected something in his personal life, like his job or a relationship. Or maybe he just wanted to make sure I didn't have a chance to win the Cedar Lake Tournament.

"You're thinking again," Carla said.

I pulled open the door at the lodge and shook my head. "Sorry. Just trying to figure out why Smudge is out to get me."

"My guess is he doesn't like you."

"Well that's hard to believe," I smirked.

"Then maybe he doesn't like dogs."

"More believable I suppose. I was thinking he's probably jealous of my ravishing girlfriend."

"Why Mr. Gordon," she said and tossed her hair. "Whoever do you mean?"

There were several tables available in the dining room and we sat at one near a window even though there was nothing to see in the deep darkness of the lawn and the expanse of the still lake. I saw the waitress appear in the black window like a ghost as she approached our table so I turned around from the nothingness outside.

"Good evening you two," she said as she placed our menus on the table. "Mr. Double Bourbon Chess Player and Miss Martini, right?" It was Carey, the waitress from the lobby bar.

"Good memory," Carla said with a smile.

"Oh, I always remember the fun ones," she said and winked. I wasn't sure if she was winking at Carla or me though. Then she belched out her hideous giggle and I cringed.

"They have you working double duty, huh?" I asked. Maybe she wouldn't find that funny.

"Not really," she said. "This is my usual gig, but when we have events like a big chess tournament I'll help out in the bar."

"Hey now," I said.

"I'm not putting it down," Carey said. "The Cedar Lake Tournament is great for us, and it's nice when I get to meet new people."

"Well that's nice," Carla said and she introduced herself and then me.

"I'm Carey," the waitress said, "at your service. Literally. Now, how about some drinks?"

After dinner Carla and I each ordered another drink, though I changed mine to a 7&7; the double bourbon just wasn't me.

When Carey brought them to our table I asked her about the argument we'd overheard the night before between Jake and Wendy.

"That was something, wasn't it?" she said.

"Does that happen often?" I asked.

She shook her head. "Never. At least not during business hours and certainly not in the office where customers can hear."

"Do you know what it was about?"

"You're a nosy one, aren't you?" she laughed.

"Well there have been some strange things going on," I said in an effort to defend myself.

"Strange things?" Carey said.

"The murder of Dan Tilley," I said.

Carey looked at Carla. "I thought you two were from out of town. How did you know Dan?"

"Ray has been involved in a few investigations," Carla said. "And we happened to be driving by when the police went out there."

"Oh, you're the ones who got sideswiped by Aaron," Carey smiled.

We'd gone from a near miss to getting sideswiped.

"Who's Aaron?" Carla asked.

"New cop in town. You're the third accident he's had."

"How'd you know about that?" I asked.

She shrugged. "Small town. Word gets around pretty quick when something big happens. So you're what, some kind of detective?"

I shook my head. "I wouldn't say that. I've been in the wrong place at the right time is all."

"And solved three murders the police couldn't," Carla added. I looked at her and she winked.

"You think Jake and Wendy's row had something to do with Dan's murder?" Carey asked. She looked as though she'd caught me in a lie; disbelief was stamped on her face like a mask.

I shrugged. "Doubtful. But anything out of the ordinary — which you say it is — can mean something. You're right, it's probably nothing. Things like that just catch my attention."

"So you're *on the case*?" She wiggled her fingers as air-quotes.

I was mid-sip and shook my head. "I wouldn't say that either, but I do have a friend who lives here so let's call me an interested party."

"Who's your friend?"

"Perry Whitton."

"Ah," she said.

Carla looked at her and cocked her head. "Ah?"

Carey shrugged. "You going to be around later?"

"We have a quick errand to run, but we'll be back in an hour or so."

She nodded. "Jake said dinner's on us tonight. Can't wait to hear the story behind *that*," and she walked away.

16

■ Businesses that cater to the needs and whims of people with pets will get my money every time. They either completely understand our needs and are, therefore, happy to oblige us with long hours of operation and tons of merchandise, or they know we pet people are total suckers. It's a toss-up. I know I'd do anything for Morphy so I am aware that I am, on a certain level, a sucker for dog stuff. But I have needs for my dog as well. When we'd come back from our hike I figured Smudge would be looking for us so I bypassed the lodge and drove straight into town where I'd seen *Camp Yip-N-Yap*, a doggy day care open 7am until midnight. Plenty of time for us to have dinner, let Smudge and Jake forget about the afternoon and then we could pick up Morphy and bring him home under cover of darkness.

We were back in our cabin at 11:30 and Morphy made a quick tour of the place, giving everything a sniff and wag of his tail until he finally leapt onto the bed to claim it as his own.

"How late do you think Carey meant when she asked if we'd be around later?" Carla asked.

"Don't know. Maybe we should stroll up to the lodge and see if she's waiting for us."

"Stroll? Did you just say *stroll*?"

"Sure. Doesn't it feel like a stroll when we go up there?"

She draped her arms over my shoulders and kissed me. "That's one of the things I love about you. You know how to use archaic words."

"Archaic? Stroll?" It was a topic I thought could certainly bear further discussion but her arms were still around my neck, my hands were on her waist and I wasn't going to miss a romantic opportunity by talking about the historic lexicology of the word 'stroll.'

Carla kissed me again and I was just about to tell Morphy to get off the bed when someone knocked on the door. "What the…? We just can't get lucky," I said.

"You've gotten lucky plenty of times, mister," she smiled. "And don't worry, your *luck* isn't going to run out any time soon." She gave me a wink and nodded toward Morphy.

In the bedroom I held my palm up as a sign for Morphy to stay put and be quiet while Carla answered the door. The cabin was small enough to hear a whisper from around the corner, but even with the bedroom door closed, I knew who Carla had let inside. "Oh, hi," I heard Carla say as if she were welcoming an old friend. "We were just wondering if we should come up to the lodge to see if you were there."

Carey, the waitress who thought my friendship with Perry Whitton warranted an *ah* comment. By asking us at dinner if we were going to be around later, I hoped she meant to explain what she'd meant. It was the second time someone had not reacted well to Perry's name. The first was Rusty Melman. He'd said something about Perry not wanting the werewolf myth to be lifted from Jasper. I'd found it an odd thing to say then and chose to ignore it, but when the waitress had offered up her *ah* in an oh-I-see manner coupled with a nod of her head, I thought it might need looking into. Not that I suspected Perry of anything, but I only knew him as a chess player and tournament organizer, a pretty narrow window into someone's psyche.

I looked at Morphy and put my finger to my lips and then showed him my palm again as I moved toward the door. He sighed and laid his head on the bed between his paws; he didn't get to meet the stranger.

I stepped into the living room and shut the door behind me. Carla and Carey were sitting across from one another, both on the edge of their seats with their elbows on their knees. They looked at me and Carla said, "Coffee or wine? We weren't sure which you'd prefer."

"Coffee sounds good," I said. "Want me to make a pot or run up to the lodge and get them to go?"

"A pot here is fine with me," Carey said.

I nodded and went about making the brew and they kept on with the chit chat.

Carla: "So where are you from?"

Carey: "Here. Born and raised. How about you?"

Carla: "Seattle. Both of us. Have you ever left?"

Carey: "I went to college in Portland and stayed for twelve years."

Carla: "You went to college for twelve years?"

They both laughed and I worried Morphy might start to howl at the sound of Carey's ratcheting guffaws. I had yet to decide if it was charming or just heinous.

Carey: "No, after I graduated I worked in an ad agency doing design and photography."

I sat next to Carla and said, "Coffee's on. Should be just a few minutes."

"Thanks, Ray," Carla said

I looked at Carey. "What made you come back?"

"Homesick mostly." She shrugged and looked at the table.

Since she glanced away when she gave me her reason I was sure there was a deeper issue than being homesick, but it was really none of my business so I didn't push. Instead I sat back and asked her what she meant when I mentioned Perry Whitton at dinner.

She sat back in her chair too and smiled. "First you tell me how you got a free meal out of Jake."

Carla and I looked at each other and she shrugged. "One of the players doesn't like me much," I told Carey.

"The one who punched you?" she asked.

"Yeah, him. He keeps telling Jake I have a dog in the cabin so I'll get kicked out." Then Carla and I both told her how we'd come home earlier and Jake searched our car and flower bed because Smudge had seen evidence of a dog. "When he didn't find anything Jake apologized for the harassment and offered us dinner." I looked at Carla as if to verify the tale but her eyes were pointed down at the coffee table. I knew what she was thinking and she was right; we'd have to pay for the dinner since we were, in fact, breaking the rules. I nodded at her and then turned to our guest. "Coffee is ready. How do you like it?"

"One sugar please."

I stepped into the kitchenette and poured coffee into three chunky mugs, spooned a little sugar into each and returned to the living room. Once we'd all taken a test sip I looked at Carey and said, "Your turn."

She shrugged. "It's nothing really. Everybody loves Perry, except for one thing."

"Which is…what?" Carla asked. She scooched to the edge of the couch and held her cup tightly with both hands.

"The whole werewolf story. I'm sure you've heard of it."

I lifted our copy of *Werewolves of the Western United States* off the end table and read the inscription out loud. *"To Carla, Did myth make the man or did man make the myth? Yours in lycanthropic research, Dr. Franklin Thuringer."* I even pronounced it correctly.

"Wow. Quite the academic," Carey said. "So you've read it?"

Carla nodded. "Not all of it, but about Jasper."

"The whole werewolf thing is kind of ridiculous. I was a little kid when all that came about, but most people today would rather forget it. Except Perry. He wants to use the myth as a tourist attraction. I mean, a girl was brutally murdered out in the woods, someone joked about it being the work of a werewolf and he wants to capitalize on that? It's in bad taste is what I think."

I remembered Perry had mentioned wanting to show me something the night Carla and I had dinner with him. He'd said he wanted my opinion on something. I wondered if had to do with the Jasper werewolf. "It was a long time ago," I said, "and I understand the family moved away."

"True on both counts," Carey said with a nod, "but I remember when it happened, everyone was scared and sad at the same time. I was in the same class as Cindy's little brother. Strange to be talking about him again. Anyway, it was one of those horrible things that affected the whole community; it changed us and brought us together. I don't think something as awful or as meaningful as that should be packaged into marketing material."

"Amen to that," Carla said. She raised her cup and took a sip.

"Do most people in town agree with you about Perry?"

"No. I imagine most of the business owners are on board with him. It's about tourism, bringing in money to keep the town alive, so I don't think anyone is against Perry, just the topic. Nobody is up in arms over it anyway."

I nodded and it was quiet as we savored our coffee and pondered the kinds of people who would be drawn to a small town famous for the alleged murder of a teenaged girl by a werewolf.

There was something more, though. I'd prompted our new friend with the question about Perry. She had hesitated a moment and then she challenged me to tell my free dinner story first. It had given her time to switch gears. I raised my eyebrows at her. "So? What did you want to come and talk to us about?"

She smiled shyly. "Actually, I'm wondering now if I should even bother, but I guess I'm here so what the hell. But before I say anything you have to know that I love Jake and Wendy as if they were my own; I would never say or do anything to hurt them."

"But...?" I prompted.

"But you asked what their fight was about and I heard something that might be important, but more likely it's nothing."

"Have you talked to the police about it?"

"Nope."

"Why not?"

"They didn't ask, you did. And like I said, it's probably nothing."

"Okay. What did you hear?"

"Most of their argument was garbled; they were trying to keep it down and the door was closed, but I heard a couple of sentences when Wendy really freaked out. 'You did what?' was one, and then a little later I heard her say, 'I can't believe you did that. I told you I didn't want any part of it.' And then Jake said, 'I had to'."

"Well..." Carla said and sighed. "It sounds like that could be about anything, really."

I looked at her. "True. You could drop almost any subject in the middle of those snippets and it might make sense. But given what has happened, and that they knew Dan Tilley, it doesn't sound good, does it?" Carla shook her head. "Is that all?" I asked Carey. She nodded. "And you're sure you don't know what they were arguing about?"

"No. They got quiet again after that."

"Do you know if Jake and Wendy were good friends with Dan Tilley, or did they just know him?"

Carey shook her head. "I think they were around the same age. What do you think about all of it?"

"Like you said, whatever they were arguing about could be completely unrelated to the murder, but those things you heard... Maybe Jake was telling Wendy what he'd done." And Jake had done *something*. His big-man-on-campus attitude certainly lent itself to Jake going behind his wife's back. The question that needed to be answered was what was he willing to do?

"The lodge isn't doing well financially," Carey offered.

"They could have been talking about the books, sure." I nodded. "Maybe Jake *had to* put the month's earnings on a football game thinking he could make up some debt if his team won, something like that. It's possible, but I'll still have to see if Dan Tilley was more than an acquaintance, or connected to the lodge somehow."

"Okay," Carey said, "but please don't go to the police if you don't have to. Overall they're good people."

"Overall?"

"If you haven't already noticed, Jake can be a bit…arrogant."

Arrogance was one thing, but I wanted to know why he said *right* all the time. Was it an affliction of some sort? A verbal psychosis brought about by a horrible English class accident?

"Why isn't the lodge doing well?" Carla asked.

Carey shrugged. "Most of the guests are people who've been here before. I don't think Jake and Wendy really advertise heavily so it's only once in a while when we get guests who've never been here. I wasn't lying when I said we like having the annual chess tournament. It's one of the few times we're completely booked up."

"Is it in danger of closing?"

"I don't know, but there are only a couple of full-time waitresses. Wendy hires temps during holidays and big events."

"Which are you?" I asked.

"Both." Carey smiled. "I'm one of the full time waitresses but I also get extra hours when it gets busy."

We chatted for another hour, mostly get-to-know-you stuff like what it was like to live in a small town of a couple thousand residents compared to a thrumming city of millions like Seattle (culture shock); where people who live on a lake go for vacation (the desert); and typical job-related questions. "What is it about chess that makes you play and teach, Ray?" Carey asked.

"Bobby Fischer said *chess is life*."

"And he is?"

My mouth dropped open and I stared at our guest. How was I supposed to respond to that? Not knowing who Bobby Fischer was, was like not knowing of Babe Ruth, Neil Armstrong, or…I took a deep breath. "He was the first American to become the World Chess Champion. In 1972 at the height of the Cold War he beat Boris Spassky of the Soviet Union. *Chess is life*. That works for me."

"I'm not sure I understand," Carey said.

"Chess has everything—"

"Here we go," said Carla. She smiled at Carey as if to say, "You asked for it."

"I'll keep it short," I said. "Chess has a beginning, a middle and an end. It gives you millions of options so you have choices to make and there are consequences to those choices, some good, some not. You need to plan, to think ahead and also see what's coming at you. Play safe sometimes, rush forward others. *Chess is life*."

"Wow," Carey said. "I've always thought it was just a game." She snorted back a laugh.

Me too, Carla mouthed silently.

"I saw that." I stood up and stepped into the kitchenette to retrieve the coffee pot. There was enough for one more cup each. As I turned back to the living room, I spied my wallet on the counter and picked it up. After filling the three mugs, I handed Carey seventy dollars.

"What's this for?" she asked.

"Tonight's dinner."

"Jake said it was on the house."

I shook my head. "Choices and consequences," I said.

Carey frowned in confusion and I looked at Carla. She shrugged noncommittally. "The thing is, Carey—"

That's when we heard a woman scream.

17

■ Carla was the first out the door, I was right behind her
and Carey followed me. Carla pointed toward the lawn
between the lodge and the lake. "I think I saw someone
over there."

I opened the passenger door of the Land Cruiser
and fished the flashlight out of the center console. The
scream had sounded like a woman but I wasn't positive.
What I was sure about was that it wasn't playful, like a
young woman and her boyfriend roughhousing and
laughing before he tries to grab her waist and instead
accidentally pulls her pants halfway down. What I'd heard
was an emotional scream, a reflexive release of shock. As I
shut the door of the car we heard another scream, but this
time it was a word, *Help!*

"Ray?" Carla started.

"I'm going to go see."

"Me too," Carey said quickly.

Carla nodded. "We both are."

"Okay," I said. "Stay close."

I kept the flashlight off and we quick-walked toward the lodge and then veered right toward the lawn. A mist had crept up from the lake and swept across the grass and swallowed the bottoms of the trees. It was almost organic in how it moved, feeling its way along the ground. I shivered, but it wasn't from the cold. We slowed our pace and then I stood still and held up my hand. "Why'd we stop?" Carey whispered.

I nodded toward the lodge and said, "Look up there, to the left." There were two flashlight beams bobbing in the air and making bright wispy circles in the mist. At first I thought there were only two people, but as the flashlights bounced I counted three other figures, two between the light bearers and another following behind. The scene reminded me of the black and white horror movies from the 1930s and 40s. *No wonder they came up with the werewolf bit.* "Follow me," I said out loud.

I led Carla and Carey across the dirt road between the cabins and the lawn. Then we stopped again and huddled behind one of the thick-trunked sequoias. "What do you think is going on?" Carla whispered.

I looked at my watch and pressed the tiny button to illuminate the face. It was just a few minutes before 1am. "Are nocturnal activities a regular thing around here?" I asked Carey.

"Not that I know of."

"Jake! Not my Jake!"

"That was Wendy," Carey said and she went around the tree and into the night.

I snapped on the flashlight, grabbed Carla's hand and said, "Come on!" We raced across the grass and caught up to the waitress about ten yards from where the people who'd come from the lodge had stopped. They stood in a semicircle and the two flashlights were trained on something low, but not on the ground. After a few more steps we were upon them and I moved ahead enough to keep Carla behind me.

I stood at the open end of the semicircle and saw what everyone else was staring at. A plastic lawn chair was overflowing with the lifeless body of a very large man. His neck was raggedly slashed open, and thick, bright blood soaked the plaid shirt and jeans. His expressionless eyes were half-open and seemed to be staring out at the lake, and what skin that could be seen through the blood spatter was gray, like a bloated fish.

I pointed my flashlight beam at the ground and turned to Carla. "You okay?" She nodded and stepped closer. I glanced at the other people in the group, five in all, but couldn't make out any details. Wendy was the only one I recognized and she was leaning heavily on a young woman. I assumed two men carried the flashlights based on their height but couldn't make out the fifth person who was just a shadow. "Who screamed earlier?" I asked.

"I did," the young woman supporting Wendy said. She looked between twenty-five and thirty-five years old and had her blond hair styled in a ponytail. She wore jeans and a dark hooded sweatshirt jacket. The mist covered her feet but I guessed she was wearing sneakers or boots. "Sorry. It freaked me out."

"Nothing to be sorry for," I said and glanced again at the body. "Anyone know what happened or see anything?"

"Who are you?" a man asked and the dark world I was standing in suddenly turned blindingly white.

I held up my hand to shield my eyes. "Get that flashlight out of my face. My name's Ray Gordon." I fumbled for Carla's hand. "We're guests here and heard the scream."

"I was coming back from a walk," the young woman said.

"In the dark?" one of the men accused.

The woman shrugged. "I couldn't sleep. That's not a crime is it?" The flashlight beam was no longer in my eyes, but I couldn't make out any detail. Every shape looked like it was cut out of black construction paper and floated above the ground. "Anyway, I saw him sitting still and thought he'd fallen asleep. Until I got close."

"Has anyone called the police?" I asked.

"Yes," said a man's voice behind one of the flashlights.

"Are you okay, Wendy?" Carey asked.

Wendy Humboldt had been quietly leaning into the young woman since we'd arrived. My eyes were getting their night vision back and I saw her nod. "Better," she said shakily.

"Why did you think this was Jake?" I asked. Her gaze floated toward me. "I heard you shout his name. You were scared it was him."

Wendy tilted her head at the young woman. "She said it was a big man who was dead. Jake's not home. Haven't heard from him for hours."

It was after one in the morning and Jake hadn't been home for hours. If he was a teenager nobody would think twice about it, but Jake was a lodge owner with customers in their rooms. And two people had been murdered within the last few days… "Where's the other one?" I said.

"The other one what?" asked Wendy.

"Five people came down from the lodge after the first scream. Two had flashlights." The two flashlight holders were still there and Wendy and the young woman made four. They all looked around but no one else was nearby. "Do any of you remember the other person?"

"Was it a man or a woman?" Carla asked.

All four of them shook their heads or shrugged. The man who hadn't shined his light in my face said, "I think it was a guy, but I'm not sure. Me and Tim were grabbing flashlights after we heard her scream and we were out the door when she came in for help."

The urgent wail of a police siren came across the lake. "Does anybody know who this is?" Carla asked and waved at the body.

I looked at Carla and then the rest of the group. "I do," I said. "It's Cal Pederson. I played chess with him this morning."

18

One squad car slowly drove onto the lodge grounds and then eased to a stop as near to us as possible, once we waved our flashlights to show where we were. The cop who got out was Aaron Anderson, the rookie who'd smashed the row of mailboxes and vomited over the porch railing along with the EMT at the Dan Tilley murder scene. He clicked on his own flashlight and ambled over to us like we were standing around an illegal campfire on the beach. "Alright folks," he drawled, "I'm sure you're just having a little fun, but making prank 9-1-1 calls is a serious offense."

I'd never heard of anyone making a prank call about a dead body. Maybe that's what teenagers in Jasper did when they were bored. I shook my head and pointed my flashlight beam at Cal Pederson's pasty dead face. "Not exactly a false alarm, Officer," I drawled back at him.

Anderson's eyes widened and he fumbled his radio off its shoulder clasp. "I've got a 12-49A out at Cedar Lake Lodge. Looks like a homicide…lots of blood. Send the coroner and wake up Lieutenant Pitt! Code three! Code three!"

It was a long night. The police kept everyone shivering at the scene for over an hour to ask questions. Lt. Pitt pulled me away from the group when it was my turn to be interrogated. "Where do I know you from?" he asked, his hand gripping my elbow as he steered me toward his squad car.

"Ray Gordon, Lieutenant. I'm the one who was at the scene a couple of days ago. Your new guy almost hit my car."

Pitt nodded. "Okay. Yeah. That's right. What're you doing here?"

"I'm in the chess tournament. Staying in cabin six." My arms were wrapped around my chest so I pointed my chin at Carla's and my temporary abode.

"Nice place?"

I shrugged. "Sure."

"Okay, tell me what happened."

I told him what I knew, which wasn't much. I didn't know Cal beyond meeting him across the board. I hadn't seen him since our chess game and I hadn't seen or heard any sort of violence leading to the murder. My involvement was all after the scream that had drawn us outside. I did recount seeing the person in the group from the lodge, who later vanished once everyone was circled around the corpse.

"Can you describe this person?" Pitt asked.

I shook my head. "When I first saw them they were all shadows and flashes of clothing. When we made it to where they were standing, the big guy, Tim I think his name is, shined his flashlight in my eyes and I was blind for a good one to two minutes. You know, where you just see that spot? Anyway, once I could see again I realized there was one fewer person than there had been. They all thought it was a man, but no one knew who he was."

"Anything else?"

"No. Not that I can think of."

Carla and I made it back to the cabin a little around 2:45am and compared notes about the questions we'd been asked. The rookie cop had interviewed her but hadn't asked any off-the-wall questions or anything that she thought could shed some light on the murder. She hadn't brought up the disappearing act of one of the group and Officer Anderson didn't ask. I wondered if I'd been the only one to think he was important.

"What do you think happened?" Carla asked.

We were lying on the bed with Morphy between us and the lights out. It felt like we were telling ghost stories at a slumber party. We petted Morph while we talked and more than once he grumbled, probably wanting us to be quiet and go to sleep. "I don't think it's a coincidence that he and Dan Tilley were similarly slashed."

"Similarly slashed? That's a tongue twister."

"Seriously."

"Seriously similarly slashed. Seriously similarly slashed. Seriously similarly slashed." She laughed.

"I think you're in shock."

She stopped giggling. "I'm sorry. That was so inappropriate. Cal wasn't as torn up as the first guy though."

"True. Maybe the killer didn't have time to finish the job. What was the girl's name? The one who found him?"

"Jenny."

"Maybe Jenny came back from her walk and spooked him."

"Wendy looked horrible, didn't she? I can't imagine being told there was a body outside and thinking it was you. How awful."

"Did they find Jake?"

"Not as far as I know."

"Did you lock the door?"

Carla reached over Morphy and slapped my arm. "Don't try to scare me."

"I'm serious. You asked me what I thought so I'll tell you. I don't know what happened exactly, but I do think there was a killer standing around with us out there and I also think he's staying in the lodge."

Carla nodded, rolled over and got out of bed. "Door's locked!" she called from the living room.

19

■ The next morning arrived like a rock through the window. Shocking and joltingly fast after the long night we'd had. Carla, even though she didn't need to, got up with me and we hustled up to the lodge for a quick breakfast.

The dining room was abuzz with chatter of Cal Pederson's demise and while Carla and I quietly ate our scrambled eggs, we heard rumors ranging from the absurd (werewolf) to the ridiculous (suicide due to being knocked out of the chess tournament). I winced when I heard the suicide theory because it was a double elimination tournament and I'm the one who handed Cal his second loss. But the rumors were just that. Obviously the lodge guests had heard what happened but they hadn't seen the body. The only way I could think of for someone to cut their own throat the way Cal's was would be to lie on the ground with a running chainsaw and…

I put my fork down and pushed away my plate of hash browns smothered in ketchup.

"Not hungry?" Carla asked.

"Not anymore." I checked my watch. "I better get downstairs before the next round starts. You okay?"

"Sure."

Meaning, not really. "You can come down and hang out if you want."

She smiled. "I wouldn't want to distract you."

"Please, distract me."

"Maybe I'll wander down after another cup of coffee."

I gave her a quick kiss and went in search of Perry Whitton. Besides having the pairings for the next round of play, I was curious to hear his take on Cal Pederson's murder. Perry was tight with many of the town who's who and he may have heard if there was a lead in the investigation.

He was at the same place I'd found him the day before, at the bulletin board posting the pairing list for the next round of play. As soon as he saw me, Perry grabbed my elbow much like Lt. Pitt had the night before, and turned me toward the back of the room. "You *saw* Cal's body?" he whispered.

"How did you know that?"

"Wendy told me."

"Wendy? When did she tell you? Do you know if Jake is back yet?"

He shook his head. "She's really worried too. No one's seen him since yesterday. Hey, after your game this morning you need to go talk to Bill Blunt, you know, the Chief of Police."

"What? Why?" Given the silent dismissal I'd received before, I was pretty sure I didn't make the short list of Chief Blunt's *Tourists of the Year*. Why would he want to see me? An image of a dentist with rusty drills and a miner's hat surfaced and I closed my eyes. An appointment with the psycho dentist actually sounded better.

"He wants to ask about Cal," Perry said. "I told him what I could over the phone, but he wants to *see* you." We stared at one another for a moment then Perry smiled.

"He's still pissed at me, isn't he?" I asked.

"From what I heard about your meeting, probably, but don't worry about it. Okay, go find your board; I need to get this round going."

My opponent was Leonard Nail, a retiree from a small town in Washington. He and his wife had come to Cedar Lake long ago on vacation and he knew then this would be where he'd retire.

"It is nice," I said. "This is my first time playing in the tournament, really like it so far. How long have you lived here?"

"Four years now. First time playing in the tournament for me, too. Thought it sounded fun, but some of you guys are pretty serious. I lost my first game and barely won my second." I raised my eyebrows and tried not to look like Nosferatu ogling my next victim.

From the front of the room Perry cleared his throat and said, "You may start your clocks."

Leonard and I shook hands and he slapped the plunger to start my time running. I brought my pawn to the e4 square, hit my plunger to stop my clock, start his and then sat back.

By the time we'd played through the opening moves, Carla had appeared at the bottom of the stairs and caught my eye. I smiled and glanced toward an empty board where no one was sitting. She nodded, moved to sit down and I looked back down at the board.

I concentrated on the game as much as I could but my thoughts drifted back and forth like a tide. *Why did Chief Blunt really want to see me? Does Leonard think I can't see what that Bishop is up to? Where is Jake Humboldt? I'm only four moves away from winning. Why would somebody kill Dan Tilley and Cal Pederson? How are they connected? And there it is!*

"Well I'll be," Leonard said. I didn't have to say *checkmate*, he could see it. "You're one of the serious ones," he said as we shook hands.

"I'm afraid so." I grinned and then pushed my mouth into a flat line. "Good game, Leonard. Really."

As Leonard trudged up the stairs I gave Perry a copy of my score sheet and let him know I won. When I turned around Carla was standing right behind me. "That was fast," she said.

"Was it?"

She smiled. "You big bully. You slaughtered him, didn't you?"

"I did. I really did. I almost feel bad about it too, he was a nice guy."

"Well what do we do now? You usually take a couple of hours, not less than one."

"How would you like to go into town? I happen to be wanted by the police."

"Why? What did you do now?"

"There's that biting wit I love so much." I smiled. "Chief Blunt would like to speak to me about Cal Pederson."

Chief Blunt made us wait for about fifteen minutes before he sent someone out into the lobby to retrieve us. I would have been mad — which I'm sure was Blunt's intention — except Tommy Ryder called and made better use of the time.

"Hi ya, Tommy," I said when I answered his call. "I'm guessing you were successful as usual?"

"Hey, I know when you're buttering me up, Ray. You will owe me for this one and I will collect, but yes, I was able to gather some intel on this guy, Thuringer." Tommy pronounced the name correctly and over-enunciated each syllable. I knew he'd found something good. "For a professor, or whatever he is," Tommy said, "this guy is some piece of work."

By the end of Tommy's report a young man whose acne-covered face looked like the sunburned surface of the moon, appeared through the door we'd seen before labeled *Authorized Personnel Only* and asked us to follow him. He ushered us into the chief's office without another word and shut the door as he left.

Chief Blunt stood up and nodded at Carla. "Miss Caplicki, if I remember right."

"Yes," Carla said. "How are you this morning, Chief?"

"Well, we'll see. Mr. Gordon."

"Chief." We shook hands and he waved us into seats. "You're okay with Carla sitting in?"

"I am. Miss Caplicki was one of the seven witnesses."

"Eight," I said.

"Well we'll get to that. I hope you're going to be more forthcoming with your information this time."

I nodded. "Whatever I can do to help." The Chief seemed to be in a better mood, and since Tommy had given me the information I needed, I thought I'd make good on my end of the deal. No reason not to really; it's not like I needed to keep things secret.

He raised his eyebrows. "Does that mean you're now going to share with me what you wouldn't when we first met?"

"If you're still interested, sure."

"We have a second body, Mr. Gordon. A second *victim*. I'm interested in everything."

I was wrong, Blunt was *not* in a better mood. I glanced at Carla and she shook her head almost imperceptibly. "Of course. Sorry," I said. Blunt had made us wait and I was being childish by trying to return the favor. I knew the Chief of Police would still want to hear what I wouldn't tell him before because everything in a murder investigation is pertinent—I'd just thrown that mantra at Carey the waitress the night before. I shrugged. "My initial thought the other day was to look at Dr. Thuringer." I made a point to pronounce the hard g.

Blunt raised his eyebrows. "The werewolf book guy? Why?"

"It was just an idea. Killings linked to a werewolf myth and a book about werewolves. How do you create sales? By having another gruesome murder that can be blamed on the werewolf. People are scared and interested and want information, and oh, look, here's a book about werewolves right here in your town!"

"Sales would have to be phenomenal to be worth it, wouldn't you think?" Chief Blunt said.

"Maybe it's not about the money as much as about being right, about being *the* authority on the subject." I did think Thuringer came across as an academic snob at the signing. He was bored as soon as I dared ask a question.

The chief nodded and rubbed his chin.

"Arrogance, huh? I'd buy that one over the book sales thing. I suppose it's plausible anyway. Are you going to tell me why you didn't tell me this the other day?"

"I didn't want to throw Thuringer under the bus just because my first impression of him wasn't the best. I wanted to check him out first."

"*Check him out*? Do I want to know any more?"

I shrugged. "I know a guy who is very good at finding information. All above board." I looked at Carla. *Right?* I mouthed. She shrugged. "Anyway, he couldn't find a criminal record for Dr. Franklin Thuringer, but he did discover an interesting academic record. Thuringer has a PhD in Anthropology and was a professor for several years but was denied tenure twice before he was let go from a university in Washington State. He landed at a community college and was let go from there after three years. Another community college hired him and then dismissed him after only one year. He's now teaching high school Social Studies at a small town south of here. His wife left him after the first community college and he is still single."

"Why did he keep getting fired?" asked Carla.

"Tommy couldn't confirm because the employers he talked to just gave confirmation of the dates Dr. Thuringer worked for them. However, and this is the fun part, most of his former supervisors hinted that all of Dr. Thuringer's misfortunes have to do with his infatuation with werewolves. The book he's been signing in your local bookshop isn't the first time he's published something on that topic."

Chief Blunt nodded while he wrote on a notepad. "Okay," he said and put his pen down, "let's talk about Cal Pederson."

Just as I'd thought, Chief Blunt wanted to know how Cal had taken his second loss and subsequent elimination from the Cedar Lake Chess Tournament. "He was actually in a pretty good mood," I said. "Our game was a lot of fun. From a chess perspective he was very proud of himself, and he had a right to be. He played very well."

"But he lost."

I smiled. "One of my own favorite games is one that I lost. I played well but it didn't turn out. I learned a lot from that game."

"Did he talk about anything else? Did he seem distracted or preoccupied?"

"No. In fact he said now that he was done with the tournament he could just enjoy the rest of the week off."

Blunt jotted some more notes on his pad and pushed his chair back. "Okay. That's all I have…"

"Eight witnesses," I said.

Blunt nodded and scooted his chair back up to his desk. "You are the only one who mentioned the extra person in your interviews last night," he said. "Even Miss Caplicki didn't say anything about the mysterious disappearing man."

"It was very late," Carla said, "and I imagine everyone was scared or shocked or something, you know? Ray's right. There was another person there initially, but our attention was on the body. I didn't see him leave."

"Him?" Chief Blunt said. "Are you sure it was a *him*?"

Carla shook her head. "No, I'm not sure."

"Okay. I'll have the witnesses questioned again," he said.

"You probably won't get any new answers," I offered. "We both know how shoddy the memory of an eyewitness can be, especially late at night."

He nodded but didn't say anything. Maybe we were finally getting on the same page.

"Chief, have you heard anything about Jake Humboldt?" Carla asked.

"Yes I have as a matter of fact. He called his wife earlier this morning. He's in Montana. Got there before he realized he never let her know where he was going. Just ran out of here and left, I guess."

"Ran out of *here*?" I asked and pointed at the floor.

Chief Blunt nodded. "Jake and I go way back. He was in here yesterday afternoon having a cup of coffee like we're apt to do on occasion. I had the crime scene photos from Dan Tilley's place on my desk. Didn't mean to have them out in front of a civilian, but…" He shrugged. "Jake looked at one of them long and hard and when I told him what it was he turned white and wide-eyed and ran outta here without a word."

"Really?" I said. "Which photo?"

The chief stared at me long enough to make me wonder if he was an open-eyed narcoleptic. Then he blinked, pulled open a desk drawer and lifted out a manila folder. "How's your Russian?" he asked as he flipped through the pictures.

"Excuse me?"

"Can you read or speak Russian?"

"No. I know a few Russians and I know a few phrases, but no, I can't read it."

Blunt closed the folder and laid a photo on the desk. Carla and I leaned forward. The picture was taken in a different room than where Dan Tilley's body was found. I remembered the photos Gabe Anderson had shown me on his phone, and the walls were a different color. The picture the chief showed us was of one wall. The top of a beige sofa lined the bottom and the lower corner of a framed painting was askew toward the top right; the subject though, was a message written in Russian: завтра прибыл. I thought it would have been scrawled in the victim's blood, but instead the letters were penned in black marker, though not very neatly, as they were spread over the width of the wall.

"What does it say?" Carla asked.

Blunt sat back in his seat and laced his fingers over his belly. "Tomorrow has come."

20

■ *"Tomorrow has come,"* I said aloud once Carla and I had left City Hall and were on the small streets of Jasper.

"What do you think it means?" Carla asked.

I shrugged. "No idea. Could be anything really: some nut-job being apocalyptic or maybe the killer warned Dan the day before."

"And do you think the killer is Russian?"

"Not necessarily. But I have no doubt it's significant."

"Which? The phrase or that it was written in Russian?"

"Both."

It was close enough to lunchtime that we decided to stop in Kathy's Café. Rusty Melman looked up from his back corner booth and Carla and I both waved. He nodded once and then looked to his right and back at me.

"Look who's sitting over there," I said to Carla before we sat down. I nodded my head in the same direction Melman had.

"Oh, they let Gabe out. That's good. I suppose it helped his case that the second murder took place while he was in jail."

"Couldn't have hurt, that's for sure. I bet there was more than that though. His mom is all smiles, but Dad doesn't seem too excited."

We slid into a booth seat and I took out my cell phone. "I forgot to call Tommy about looking up Gabe."

"I was supposed to remind you after the hike. Sorry."

I shrugged. "A lot happened, we both forgot. It's okay though, they released him. Do you mind if I call Perry real quick?"

"Go for it, Mr. Investigator Man."

"How do you know I'm investigating?"

"You have that look you get, all serious and stony faced. I need to get you a fedora, then you'd look like Humphrey Bogart in *The Maltese Falcon*."

"I'll take that as a compliment."

Carla smiled and I dialed Perry's number. With no cellular phone service on the other side of the lake, which is where Perry was, the call went straight to his voicemail. I left a message asking him to get me Cal Pederson's address.

"What do you need his address for?" Carla asked.

"There's got to be a connection somehow between Tilley and Cal. I'll give it to Tommy and see if he can come up with something." I shook my head as I thought about it. "You just don't kill random people like that and leave cryptic messages in Russian."

"There wasn't a message on Cal."

"True. Unless it was in his pocket or somewhere else we didn't see and Blunt didn't tell us. Or it's like I thought before, the killer didn't have time to finish the job."

The young blond waitress who'd served us a day or two before floated up to our table. "Welcome back, you two. How's the tournament going for you, Mr. Chess Player?"

"Undefeated so far," I said.

"Wow, that's great. Do you know what you want or do you need a couple more minutes?" The menus were on the table, tucked on end between the salt and pepper shakers, but we hadn't looked at them yet.

"A couple more minutes, I think," Carla said.

I stopped the waitress before she turned and left. "Hey, do you know that kid down there?" I glanced to where Gabe looked to be finishing up his fries.

"Yeah. His name's Gabe Anderson. Kind of weird if truth be told."

"Why do you say that?"

She shrugged. "He doesn't have many friends, doesn't talk to anybody. He just got out of jail too. Just weird."

"Fair enough," I said. It could have been worse; he might have the wrong brand of cell phone. "Are those his parents?"

"Yeah. I guarantee he gets some of his weirdness from them."

I nodded as if I understood what she meant. "Thanks."

Carla and I scanned the menus. Before I could decide between a cheeseburger or a pastrami on rye Gabe Anderson moved into my peripheral vision. I set down my menu and looked up as he slowed down to look at me. He blinked once when our eyes met and he stared at me as if he was reading a sign in a foreign language and trying to figure out what it meant.

"We were at the scene of Dan Tilley's murder," I told him.

He nodded as he put two and two together. "I didn't do it."

"I never thought you did."

"Really?"

"Really."

"They arrested me though." His parents took up protective positions behind him and looked at me curiously.

I shrugged. "They don't always get it right the first time."

"Yeah." He brightened. "Maybe I'll have some street cred with the girls now," he smiled.

I thought about what the waitress had said. "Maybe."

"See ya round, then."

"See you." I nodded at his parents who'd remained silent during the conversation. His mother's eyes were rimmed in pink and were still watery. The father wore glasses with thick black frames that were popular in the 1960's and a black suit from the same era. As they walked by the mother placed her hand on my shoulder and I felt a feathery squeeze and they were gone.

"What do you suppose that was about?" I asked Carla and touched my shoulder.

"Appreciation. For believing in her son."

"Odd they didn't ask who we were."

"I'm sure he's being questioned right now. Probably not with as much gusto as the police though."

Our waitress returned and raised her eyebrows at us, one hip thrown to the side. "I'll have the Cobb salad," Carla said.

"Cheeseburger for me, please, and two iced teas." The waitress walked away without saying anything or writing down our order. "I guess she didn't like me talking to Gabe."

"Maybe she'll spit on your burger."

"Thanks."

After lunch we drove back out to Dan Tilley's house. I pulled over and crunched to a stop on the gravel shoulder out front, almost exactly where we'd been before.

"What are we doing here?" Carla asked.

"I just want to look. The police suspected Gabe Anderson of the murder. He'd shown up on his bike, remember? He said he rides this way every day, a long stretch where anyone can see him."

"Okay…"

"Well, I'm curious; did anyone see anything or anyone that day besides Gabe Anderson riding his bicycle home from school? My guess is no one did or else they wouldn't have arrested Gabe so quickly. And if that's true, how did the killer get here? If he didn't drive, how did he get here without being seen by anyone?"

"How do you know it's a *he*?"

"Touché, but I don't want to believe a woman did that."

"That's sexist."

"I know, but that's what I prefer to believe."

"You do realize that—"

"Okay, we're drifting off topic here. I'm not trying to insult your gender, I'm just hypothesizing. Now, where was I?" Carla stared at me. "Look, I'm not saying a woman isn't *capable* of committing a brutal bloody murder. I just prefer to believe the fairer sex is just that. Okay?"

"Okay. Because you better believe there are women plenty capable of killing someone like that."

"Oh, I know. I might be sitting next to one."

She punched me in the shoulder. "Watch it, bub." She smiled.

"Now then, how did the *non-gender-specific* killer get to Dan Tilley's house unseen?"

Carla shrugged and looked out at the countryside. "There have to be several ways."

I nodded. "I think Dan either knew his killer, and maybe gave him a ride to the house, or the killer came to the back of the house through the fields and trees."

"That's a long hike from town."

"Agreed. And if that's the case, it would have to be someone who knows the area pretty well."

"So where does that lead us?"

I shrugged. "I'm not sure. More questions really."

We returned to the lodge before Perry Whitton and the remaining chess players had finished for the day. I pulled over behind Perry's car and got out and Carla climbed over the center console into the driver's seat. "I'm going to get Cal Pederson's info," I told her. "Should just be a couple of minutes."

"I hope so." She winked and stepped on the gas.

Perry sat behind his table with his arms crossed over his chest. Spread out before him were scoresheets from the games of the day and an open laptop to his right. Two players sat at a board, their heads in their hands as they studied the position. The room was quiet and otherwise empty.

Perry looked up as I came down the stairs and beckoned me over; he pointed to his watch and then held his thumb and forefinger close together, meaning there wasn't much time left in the last game to finish the round. I turned a folding chair sideways, sat down and assumed a position similar to Perry, arms crossed, brooding scowl.

The man playing the black pieces, a tall Scandinavian with a bushy blond goatee and dressed like a logger, eased his hand out over the board, picked up his Rook, moved it over two squares, set it down and then stopped his clock.

The other player, a younger man in his late twenties or early thirties, and wearing a sweatshirt, crisp jeans, and work boots that had never seen a job site, remained still for only a few seconds before his hand shot out, moved his Bishop, and stopped his clock.

Then in a flurry, both men sat up straight and made the remaining moves as fast as they could. Their hands hovered above the board waiting for their clock to start and in a flash their move was made and the clock stopped again. The rules of chess stipulate that whichever hand a player uses to move a piece must also be used to touch the clock. As such, both men had one arm stretched out to their side as if for balance while the other arm jerked between the board and the clock.

They moved fast, each player anticipating what the other would do, playing tactically in the remaining seconds. There was no time for strategy. A piece landed on a square, *tap!* Then the clock was stopped for that player and started for the other, *slap!* In a matter of seconds the back and forth play repeated itself: *Tap! Slap! Tap! Slap! Tap! Slap! Tap! Slap!*

"Time!" the Scandinavian logger said.

The young man in the sweatshirt stopped his hand above the board and glanced at the clock. His flag had fallen, his time had run out and he lost the game. His shoulders rounded over and he looked back down at the board. He shook his head. "Shit."

They shook hands and the Scandinavian said, "Great game, Tate. You had me on the ropes."

Tate nodded, stood up and headed up the stairs.

Perry tapped the result of the game into his laptop and when the winner had gone up the stairs he turned to me and said, "What's up?"

"I need Cal Pederson's contact info."

"You going to send him a card? Too late, don't you think?"

"Funny. Too soon, Perry, but funny." He shrugged. "I have a guy who can do some research," I said. "I want to see if there's any relationship or commonalities between Pederson and Dan Tilley."

He nodded. "You don't think Blunt and his crew can do it?"

Tommy can do it faster, I thought. Which wasn't fair, but I was used to Tommy and his possibly questionable tactics, whereas a police inquiry is part of the bureaucratic wheel that tends to turn about as fast as Congress. "It's not that," I said. "I just think two teams working from different directions can close the gap quicker. I'll share whatever we learn with them."

"Okay. Yeah, it's no problem. He turned to his laptop and pulled up Cal Pederson's information. He wrote the address, phone number and even Cal's USCF membership number on a scrap of paper and slid it across the table.

Carla and Debbie Mathews sat on the porch of cabin five, each with a goblet of red wine in hand. "Speak of the devil," Carla said.

Debbie looked my direction as I stepped toward the cabin. "Still undefeated I hear," she said.

I shrugged. "It's been a good tournament for me so far."

"Did you play the man who was killed the other night?"

"I did. That morning in fact."

Debbie shuddered at the thought. "Are you going to win?"

"That's my plan." I smiled. "How's the fishing?"

"Good! I've caught a mess of trout and a few Kokanee; one was a sixteen-pounder."

"Sounds good. So you're going to stick around?"

She nodded. "Good fishing and an exciting chess tournament, how could I not?"

Carla looked at me. "Did you get the information you needed?"

I nodded. "Called Tommy from the front desk. We'll know more in the morning."

21

■ Carla stayed on the porch with Debbie. I declined their invitation for a glass of wine and went into our cabin to play through some tactical positions. I wasn't a solid believer in superstitions, but Debbie going on about my being undefeated in the tournament could easily have jinxed me and I wanted to keep any bad juju at bay. Tactical problems and some study time with a game of Fischer's or Capablanca would help.

I grabbed a book and took a flank position on the couch. Morphy hopped up and took what remained. Tactical problems are drills for chess. Hundreds of books are available that contain thousands of diagrams of chess positions with different instructions for the reader, find the best move for White, find checkmate in two moves, find checkmate in four moves, and so on. They're nice because the reader does not need a board and pieces to set up, just look at the diagram and solve the problem in your head. Usually the first move is a capture or a check, but not always. Some make you think a little differently.

BLACK

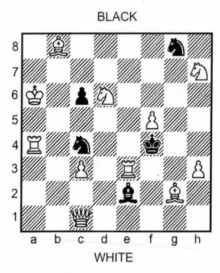

WHITE

White to move, mate in 2

I'd been looking at tactical problems for about fifteen minutes and had set up a board in preparation of studying one of Bobby Fischer's games when Carla popped through the front door. "Perry invited us over for dinner again tonight," she said. "He insisted."

"Insisted? Maybe his wife is back."

She shook her head. "I don't think so. He said there would be others there after dinner and it was important we be there, or at least you, so he was going to feed us first."

"Okay, my interest is piqued."

"I know, mine too."

"So what do we do until then?"

She smiled. "Are you done with your studies?"

"I think I am now."

She turned and went into the bedroom, pulling her shirt over her head as she went.

Dinner for me, Carla and Perry consisted of two large pies from the local pizzeria and a six-pack of beer. Not exactly a black-tie event, but the pizza was first rate.

"I would like your opinions on something," Perry said as we each lifted a second slice from the greasy cardboard boxes. "I meant to show you the other night, but the conversation went off topic."

"Sure," I mumbled around a mouthful of melty mozzarella. "What's on your mind?"

"Would you consider yourselves tourists? Not all of the time of course, but here, in Jasper, during this trip?"

Carla and I glanced at each other. I knew she was thinking the same thing as me: Perry's vision was to turn Jasper into *the* werewolf tourist destination of the Pacific Northwest. "I don't know about Ray," Carla said, "since he's here for the tournament, but I guess I think of myself as a tourist on this trip."

"Great! Can I show you something then?" We nodded and Perry jumped from his seat and trotted down the hallway and into another room. Carla and I looked at each other like we had just been locked into our seats on a carnival ride we'd been dared to try. Carey the waitress had told us what Perry had in mind for the town but now we were going to see it.

My mind raced with images of the tamest black and white still photos from *I Was a Teenage Werewolf* to the bloodiest gore-splattered movie posters of the 1980s. What did Perry have in that room that would entice people to come to Jasper?

I heard Perry coming back so I took another monster bite of pepperoni and black olive to keep my mouth fully engaged. If what he had to show us was in bad taste, I wanted to be able to formulate a good response. He came into the dining room holding a poster board with its blank backside facing us. He had a sheepish grin on his face but his eyes were clear and determined. Perry stopped at the end of the table, set the poster on it and spun it around. "What do you think?" he asked.

The image was a midnight blue starry sky with a glowing full moon at the top. Most of the poster was taken up with tall silhouetted mountains, the town of Jasper in the foreground toward the bottom, the windows of the buildings lit warmly from within, and the moon stretched out as a reflection on the lake. On the highest peak, closest to the moon, was a werewolf with its chest thrust out, arms thrown back and its head held up in a classic howling pose. Yellow and green lettering reminiscent of 1930s horror movie posters read, *Jasper, OR. Werewolf Capital of the United States! For the Beast in You!*

Carla nodded politely. "The artwork is great, Perry. Don't you think so, Ray?" I nodded and chewed slower. She bugged her eyes at me and turned back to our host. "But it might be, I don't know, a little…harsh."

"Why?" Perry asked. "There's no blood or even any implied violence."

"Well…okay. The reason there's even a werewolf myth here is because of a really violent death. I think when people hear that they might become a little turned off."

"Except the weirdos," I said. They both looked at me. "Am I wrong? They're out there, people who really get into unsolved crimes. They're fascinated by them, they study and research them. It's crazy. Think Jack the Ripper: there are groups of people dedicated to solving the case."

"Weirdos, huh?" Perry said.

"Well maybe that's not the right word. How about enthusiastic hobbyists?"

Perry tapped his finger against the poster board and stared at me and then at Carla. "I need tourists," he said, "not weirdos or *enthusiastic hobbyists*."

I shrugged. "You need the right hobbyists. Water skiers, hikers, campers, like that."

"True, and we do get those, but they don't spend enough money in town. They pack in their supplies. I'm afraid the town is dying."

The doorbell rang and Perry asked me to take the pizza boxes into the kitchen while he stashed the tourism poster and answered the door.

"How many posters do you think he already had made?" Carla asked once we were in the kitchen.

"He's probably still in the design phase. I bet there are a few more in that back room but that was his favorite."

"I hope I didn't hurt his feelings."

We heard a deep voice boom from the living room and went to see who we were there to meet. "I hope it's not Chief Blunt again," I whispered. "I've seen enough of him for a few days."

It wasn't Chief Blunt; it was Jake and Wendy Humboldt, the owners of Cedar Lake Lodge. At 6'4" Jake was the immediate focal point in the room. He wore jeans, a white button-up with a black sports jacket and loafers. Wendy was similarly dressed but wore a green blouse under a leather waistcoat and dress boots. They would have looked like a clothing ad for *Lodge Owners Today* except for Wendy. She clung to Jake and stared as if she was watching a war break out just down the street.

"Jake, Wendy," Perry said as he resumed his hosting duties, "you remember Ray and Carla? They're staying in one of your cabins."

"Of course," Jake said. He stepped forward and we shook hands. "I'm sorry I wasn't here when Mr. Pederson was killed, right? But I appreciate your handling the situation."

I made a mental note to get a psychology book and see what it meant to inexplicably turn a sentence that didn't start out as a question into a sentence that ended as a question. "I didn't really do anything, Jake," I said. "I'm glad Wendy's okay though. She had quite a scare."

He nodded and took a deep breath and the doorbell rang again.

It was Chief Blunt.

22

■ Perry directed all of us into what he called the Lakeview Room. It had fifteen foot tall windows that looked out over Cedar Lake, two leather sofas, an assortment of pillowy chairs, and tables laden with framed photos. Two walls were wrapped with bookshelves and held volumes of business and economics, history and classic literature.

Perry and Chief Blunt sat in individual La-Z-Boys while the two couples each took a sofa. We all stared at one another and out the windows before Blunt said, "What's this all about, Perry?"

"I don't believe I need to make any lengthy introductory speeches, Bill. How about we just jump into the deep end and let Jake tell us why we're here?"

Everyone's head swiveled toward Jake Humboldt and he took a deep breath. "Okay," he said, "Well, it really started when I saw that picture on Bill's desk, right?" He sat up and inched to the edge of the cushion and Wendy scooted closer to him. "I'll be honest," he paused and looked at each of us in turn, "I freaked out a little."

"Why?" Blunt asked. "Where did you run off to?"

Jake held up his palms. "I'll get to that." He looked across the table at Carla and me. "When we were in high school there was a girl, Cindy Bickerman, who everyone kind of picked on. I'm not saying it was okay, it's just the way things were back then, right? Anyway, she was…killed—"

"Murdered," Chief Blunt interrupted.

"That was never proven," Wendy said quietly.

Blunt stared at her. "It sure as hell wasn't a werewolf."

"What were you saying, Jake?" I said a little loudly.

He nodded as he got back on track. "Cindy was killed just before Halloween, like a week before. About a month or so after that, me and some of the guys I used to hang around with all got letters, right? There was no return address, it didn't even say, Dear Jake, and there were just two words. And they were in Russian."

"Russian?" I said. "You're positive?"

He nodded and pulled a yellowed envelope from his inside pocket. "We didn't have the Internet back then of course, but I was able to figure it out in the library." He held the letter out over the table to me. "This is why I went to Montana."

Chief Blunt stood up and snatched the envelope out of Jake's hand before I could reach it. "I'd like to take a look at that," he said.

While the Chief of Police sat back down and took out the letter, Jake went on. "My mom lives in Florence and still has a lot of my old stuff in storage. I hadn't thought about that letter in years, right? None of us knew who they were from or what it was supposed to be about. Then, when I saw the picture of that writing on Dan's wall and you told me what it said, I *had* to go find this."

The Chief passed the letter and envelope to me. The address was black ink and had been typed. The postmark was local and like Jake had said, there was no return address or any other distinguishing marks. The letter was a piece of notebook paper that had been cut down in order to fit inside the envelope without the need to fold it, sort of a poor man's index card. Written on the paper in black ink were two Russian words: до завтра.

"What does it say?" I asked.

"*Do zavtra*," Jake said. "It means *till tomorrow*. Of course when Bill told me the writing on Dan's wall said, *Tomorrow has come* it got my attention. You know the rest."

"No, I don't think we do," Blunt said. "Who all received the letters?"

Jake looked at the table and counted out on his fingers. "Me, Dan, Tom Davis, Gary Lombard and Doug Kincaid."

"Have you been in contact with any of those other three?"

Jake shook his head. "They all left after high school. I think I heard that Gary died some years ago, but I'm not sure about Tom or Doug."

"And you're sure when you received these letters none of you knew what they were about?" I asked. How could a group of friends, even admittedly dumb jocks, receive mysterious letters and not have a clue as to what they were about? Or who they were from? Really have no idea at all? High school student, thy name is unfocused.

Jake shrugged. "We thought it was some kind of weird joke, right? I don't remember any Russians in Jasper back then — or now for that matter — and we never played a Russian football team."

"You said you all thought it might have been a joke. From who? Any ideas at all?" Blunt asked. The chief's voice had become official and he was jotting notes on a small spiral pad he'd taken from his breast pocket. We were witnessing a police interview of sorts.

Jake said, "There were lots of groups back then, you know? We were the jocks; everyone who received those letters was on the football team. There were hippies, greasers, whatever. We thought it might have been from one of the players from a rival team, but why did only the five of us get the letter and not the whole team?"

"And why in Russian?" Blunt mused.

It sounded rhetorical to me but Jake must have thought otherwise. He said, "Russia was in the news a lot back then, what with the Cold War and all, right?"

Cold War and all I thought. "You said Cindy Bickerman was killed when you were in high school," I said. "What *year* was she killed?" I had read it in Thuringer's account, but at the moment, with what my brain was trying to cough up, I couldn't remember it.

Chief Blunt, Jake and Wendy all said in unison, "1972."

I nodded as I did the math in my head and tried to remember the details of what Jake's Cold War phrase had brought to the surface of my thoughts. "I believe you're looking for a chess player," I said aloud.

"What? Why?" Blunt spat. "You're obsessed with chess, Mr. Gordon."

"Wait a minute," I said. "Perry, back me up here. The World Chess Championship between Bobby Fischer and Boris Spassky was in 1972. It was huge news because Fischer was the first American to make it that far and he was playing the Soviets. It was very political because of the Cold War."

"Okay," Blunt said. "Jake, were you and your friends on the chess team as well as the football team?"

Jake laughed and shook his head. "No. I don't even know if there was a chess team."

Blunt looked back at me. *Any more stupidity to contribute?* he seemed to ask.

I smiled like a magician whose audience thinks they know what trick is about to happen, but he has something far more grand up his sleeve. Blunt thought I had nothing but I was about to blow his and everyone else's mind. "Chess was everywhere during the Championship," I said. "The games were reported in papers and the evening news, sets were flying off the shelves, kids were learning chess, adults were joining chess clubs and America was rallying behind Fischer like he was some sort of hero."

"What's your point, Gordon?" Blunt sighed.

"The 1972 World Chess Championship was played through the summer and ended in September, one month before Cindy Bickerman's death." Blunt opened his mouth but I held up my finger. "The first game was adjourned, I think after the 40th move."

"Adjourned?" Blunt said. "What do you mean, they quit?"

"Only until the next day. Spassky wrote his next move down and it was sealed in an envelope. The next day they would open the envelope, play the move and keep going. But here's the thing. When they adjourned, Fischer leaned over and said to Spassky, in Russian, *Do zavtra.* Till tomorrow."

23

■ "You're saying Bobby Fischer murdered Dan Tilley and Cal Pederson?" Blunt said.

"Of course not. Fischer died years ago. I think you're looking for someone who was infatuated with the World Championship, someone who was young at the time and impressionable."

"Why impressionable?" Perry asked.

"Because he used the same phrase Fischer did. I imagine when the public heard he'd said that in Russian they went wild. It sounds like something people would start to say among themselves to sound cool or hip or whatever the term was in 1972."

"Someone like you," Blunt said.

"Oh yeah, exactly like me. I would love to have witnessed that particular World Championship, but I wasn't even born yet. You guys were."

Perry and his other guests looked at one another while Carla and I sat back on the sofa. She held my hand and smiled but I wasn't sure I was happy about my revelation.

Yes, Jasper was a small town, but 1972 was a long time ago and plenty of people were enamored with Bobby Fischer's success. Who, out of the three or four thousand townspeople would single out five teenage boys and why?

Then it hit me.

"Cal Pederson's not supposed to be dead," I said and looked at Chief Blunt.

He nodded and sighed. "I was just thinking that myself. Let's hear your line of thought."

I sat back up but kept one hand on Carla's knee. "Mistaken identity. Whoever killed Cal Pederson thought he was killing someone else. It explains why the body wasn't torn up like Dan Tilley's and why there was no Russian note."

"You're assuming the murders are connected," Perry said. "Who's to say they're not a coincidence?"

I shook my head and was glad to see Chief Blunt doing the same. "At least two times I know of Cal Pederson was mistaken to be Jake. Once by me and Carla and once by Jake's own wife. In the dark they looked very similar if only because of their size. Jake's letter is the real tie, though. Dan and Jake both received the same letter in high school. That makes them connected. The Russian message at Tilley's and the murder of a Jake lookalike at Cedar Lake Lodge pretty much drives it home. Am I on track, Chief?"

"I'd say so, yes."

"Wait a minute," Wendy said. "Just what are you saying?"

I looked into her eyes and saw not fright, but sadness, as if she knew the truth of some horrible thing but was powerless to stop it, so instead tried to ignore it. "I'm saying your husband, not Cal Pederson, was the intended victim."

"But they didn't do anything! Jake just sat here and said so!" Jake eased back in his seat and wrapped his arms around Wendy and she leaned against him.

"We'll figure it out," he said.

Blunt looked at them. "I'm afraid Ray is right, Jake. I don't have a big department, but I'll offer what protection I can. In the meantime, you two might consider a vacation."

Jake shook his head. "No. We've got a full house at the lodge, right? I'm not going anywhere. Let's just figure out who's doing this. Who was here then that's here now?"

"Where do we start a search like that?" Carla asked.

"With everyone who's playing at the Cedar Lake Chess Tournament," I said. "Perry, you have everyone's addresses, right?"

He nodded.

Chief Blunt stood up and said, "Okay, I've got work to do."

The rest of us stood and looked outside at the lake.

"*Do zavtra*," Perry said. Everyone turned and stared at him.

"Too soon, Perry," I said.

24

Carla was in the shower when I woke. We'd developed
a system to get up before it was light and let Morphy
outside to do his business. It wasn't complicated, wake up
and take care of the dog. Since Carla was in the shower I
knew she'd already secreted Morphy in and out of the
cabin so I filled his water and food dishes. He sniffed at
the kibble but instead of eating jumped up on the couch to
help me check my messages.

I found it strange how I couldn't get a phone
signal at all in the area around the lodge, but text
messages seemed to get through — at least intermittently. I
had one text from Tommy Ryder: *No connection between
your vics. None. Zip. Zero. Nothing I can find anyway. No need
to call.*

I sighed and shook my head. Morphy looked at
me and raised a paw. I patted my lap and he lay down so I
could pet and tug on his ears.

After the revelation of Jake Humboldt's mysterious letter the night before I'd already concluded what Tommy had confirmed. The Russian phrase *Do zavtra*, along with the year the letters were sent, had me convinced the killer was a chess player, or if not a chess player, then someone who had been obsessed with Bobby Fischer in 1972.

For me, that meant checking the backgrounds of all the chess players in the Cedar Lake Tournament, especially those who had been around Jasper in 1972. I also wanted to look into the Jasper High School archives and see if I could get a sense of Jake Humboldt's adolescent world. He'd said he and his friends were jocks, but there were other groups of kids just as there are today. If I could get an idea of who his friends were, maybe it would help bring some of his Russian-quoting enemies to the surface.

Carla and I were having breakfast in our cabin as I relayed all of this. "And how do you plan to go about it?" she asked. "Didn't someone say we didn't have much time?"

I could not remember anybody saying that, but it was true nonetheless. "I'll need help if I want to keep playing in the tournament. Perry already said he'll provide all the info he can on the players. As far as Jasper High School in 1972…"

"Yearbooks."

"Excuse me?"

"High school yearbooks."

"Good idea. Maybe the local library has copies."

"Maybe. I'll go check while you're playing this morning."

"Really? That'd be great, but are you sure you want to?"

"If Tommy Ryder can do it, I can!" She smiled. "Anyway, it'll be exciting. Investigating in the library."

"I have no doubt you can do it," I said, "but if you really think looking for stuff in a library is exciting, I need to rethink this relationship."

"Ray!"

"No, I mean, suddenly you're way more interesting and sexier than I thought."

She laughed and *that's* how I knew, how I always knew, Carla was more interesting and sexier than anybody thought.

There were fewer chess players in the basement of Cedar Lake Lodge. Some of the players who'd been eliminated were still on the grounds enjoying a week away from their regular lives even though they'd been knocked out of the tournament. Some played speed chess at five bucks a game against Kevin Corsmo. I'd seen a couple familiar faces reading books in the lobby and some came downstairs and played casual games of chess.

I looked at the pairing sheet, saw I was playing a man named Vick Tomlinson. He was rated well below me, but was still in the tournament. I reminded myself to pay attention to the game. Underestimating an opponent was the quickest way to defeat.

Perry was at the control table and I nodded to him as I took my seat behind the white pieces on board three. My opponent sat opposite me as I was straightening and centering my men within their allotted squares. I glanced up and he gave me a nod and a tight-lipped smile. He stuck out his hand and I shook it. "Vick Tomlinson," he said.

"Ray Gordon."

"Undefeated Ray Gordon," he said.

I shrugged. Vick was probably in his early fifties, maybe late forties and had a thick, poorly cut mass of blonde hair that was silver around the temples. He wore jeans, a country music concert t-shirt and an unbuttoned flannel of a blue and green tartan pattern.

Perry stood up and gave his game-starting spiel and Vick said, "Good luck."

"Good luck to you too, Vick," I said and he started my clock.

I brought my pawn out to the e4 square, Vick responded with pawn to e5. It was a straightforward opening with millions of possibilities to follow. I played Knight to f3 and he pushed his pawn to d6. My goal was to develop my pieces quickly and control as much of the board as possible. I didn't know how much Vick played or if he was fairly casual about chess. Either way, the quicker I could assume control of the game the better.

After only a few more moves I knew I had him. By the twelfth move I already owned the white diagonals and the open d file, his black-square Bishop was useless, my Queen was in a better position than his, and I had one of his Knights pinned.

I got up and poured a cup of coffee from an urn in the back corner. The basement was quiet but for the occasional cough, scratch of pencil on paper, and the crackle of Smudge's plastic chip bag. Every time he reached for another chip the bag would scrunch and rattle and crinkle. His opponent had his hands over his ears as he studied the board and other players around the room would shoot an occasional glare over their shoulder directed at Smudge.

I told Perry I needed to run upstairs and came back with a large bowl from the kitchen. I snatched the bag of chips out of Smudge's hands and poured them all into the bowl and handed it to him. "Shh," I said.

The look on Smudge's face started as shock and then warped into anger. He started to get up, but the applause from around the room stopped him. He looked around and everyone stared back. "Sorry," he said.

I patted his shoulder, walked back over to my game and sat down. It took a half hour to get through the next three moves, but then I saw something that made my heart sing.

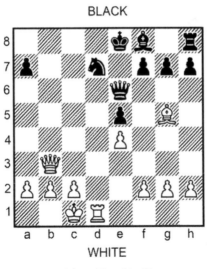

After 15. ...Nxd7

The Queen is the most powerful piece a player has, which is why it often comes under attack and must be protected. A lot of effort goes into keeping the Queen safe while also using her as an attacking piece. So, when the Queen is sacrificed in order to win the game, it is a thing of rare beauty. With my Bishop cleared from the b file, my Queen had a clear path to check Vick's King on the back rank. I moved my Queen to b8. "Check."

Vick looked over the board and sat back in his seat. "Nice," he said and tipped over his King to resign the game. The only move he had was to capture my Queen with his Knight which would leave the d file open for my Rook. Rook to d8 was checkmate because it would be protected by my Bishop on the g5 square which also guarded against the King's escape to e7. Beautiful.

The sun was still high enough in the sky that I knew I could eat a late lunch without ruining my appetite for dinner. I turned and spotted Carla sitting in an Adirondack chair out on the lodge lawn and facing the lake. I went back inside and ordered two cups of coffee.

"Hey Daphne," I said and handed her a coffee.

"Hey. Thanks. Who's Daphne?"

I dragged a chair over and sat down. "The hot girl in *Scooby-Doo*. How'd the library pan out?"

"Jinkies, Fred, not so good. The city library does not keep high school yearbooks. However I was informed that the high school library does."

I nodded. "Makes sense, I guess."

"Yes, it does. Until I was also told that the high school library isn't open to the local citizenry. Students only."

"Local citizenry?"

"Yep. Actual words. I think the librarian was a suffragette."

I smiled and burnt my tongue with the coffee. "I have an idea how we can get our hands on them," I said.

"Oh? Am I going to impersonate a new student?"

Carla looked great and I thought she could probably pull off a grad student, but high school was a stretch. A big stretch. Luckily I also knew when to keep my mouth shut. "No, I think I'll ask Gabe Anderson to get them for us."

"You think he will?"

"I do. We're pals."

She sipped her coffee and stared at me over the rim of her cup. "You haven't said anything so I'm kind of afraid to ask."

"The guy I played was good, but not great. I was really feeling it this morning too and I won, with a Queen sacrifice no less. I'll show you when we get back to the cabin."

"Nice job, mister. Can't wait." She smiled and held her paper cup toward me. I tapped mine against hers and we drank.

25

■ We elected to have our late lunch in Jasper instead of the lodge on the possibility of spotting Gabe Anderson. If we didn't see him, we had a general idea of where he lived.

"I have more research to do," I said and took a bite of my turkey on rye.

"What is it?" Carla asked. She was working her way through a bowl of clam chowder and a garden salad. We sat in a back corner booth at Kathy's Café which up to then had seemed to be the favorite hang-out in town but we'd seen no sign of Gabe Anderson and even Dr. Melman had vacated his post before we'd arrived.

I drew two sheets of folded paper from my inside jacket pocket and smoothed them out on the table. "Perry gave me all of the chess players' information. I offered to drop them off at the police station."

"Really?" Carla smirked. "You're just going to give them the list without checking any of it yourself?"

I pulled a second copy of the list from my pocket and laid it on the table. "I did some preliminary work."

"That's my man. Any standouts?"

I shook my head. "I crossed out a few who look too young to have been around in 1972."

"Does that really rule them out? What if they're just using the local history to commit crimes today?"

"It's possible, but I think the safer bet is to at least save them for last. Notice I didn't obliterate their names."

"Okay, and what do we do with this stuff?" She tapped her fork on the pages.

"We need ages, addresses — past and present — any connection with the town of Jasper or with Jake and his friends, and anything unusual."

"Unusual?"

"Suspicion of murder, armed robberies, other felonies, like that."

"Wow, who knew chess players were such a rough bunch?"

"Hopefully only one of them is."

After I left the list of chess players in the care of the Jasper Police we drove out to Dan Tilley's house but didn't stop. We drove along the straight stretch that eventually led into a pine forest. The autumn rains had yet to visit and the trees looked dry and dusty standing amid a bed of brittle needles and brush. A fire just waiting for a match.

About two miles beyond the Tilley house I spotted a mailbox on the right side of the macadam and slowed down. "Anderson," Carla read. I cranked the wheel and eased down the pea gravel driveway that twenty yards ahead veered left and vanished among the trees.

"No, this isn't creepy at all," Carla said.

"It would be if it was completely dark," I said. "There's still a little light left." I steered through the turn and then right. The trees were thick and stood close to the road sucking up what light was left in the sky. I glanced in the rearview mirror just to make sure we weren't being pushed into a trap and then made a mental note to cut back on my movie intake.

After ten more yards the trees thinned out and we saw a house. It was two storeys, painted the same greens and browns of the forest it was perched within and seemed in good repair. "At least it's not a werewolf movie house," I said. A wide porch wrapped around the front and near side and was laden with a variety of outdoor furniture.

As I pulled in front and stopped the car, Carla craned her neck and looked at the windows of the house. "I don't think anyone is home," she said.

I pointed at two mountain bikes that leaned against the porch. "Gabe is."

The boards of the porch creaked as we stepped over to the front door and it made me think of all the western movies where cowboys would clomp across the wooden sidewalks. Carla clung to my right arm with both hands and walked just behind me; I was thinking westerns, she was thinking horror movies. I rang the doorbell and we waited to see who was right.

"See?" Carla whispered. "No one is home."

I pushed the round backlit button again and this time the door swung inward. Gabe Anderson stood on the threshold and held the door with one hand. He wore the gray stocking cap we'd seen when we first met him, baggy jeans, lime green skater shoes and a white t-shirt. There was blood on it. Not a lot, but little spatterings of bright red. Carla's grip on my arm tightened and I hoped the drops were just ketchup.

"Oh, hey," Gabe said.

"Hi Gabe. Do you remember us?"

"Yeah. What's up?"

"Is everything okay?"

"Sure."

"Great. Do you have a minute? I'd like to talk to you about something."

He glanced over his shoulder and then back at us. "Yeah, I guess. Come on in."

We stepped inside and Gabe closed the door. The living room was tastefully decorated with a leather sectional and two matching recliners that surrounded a wide coffee table. Two floor lamps were dark but I could still make out a classic fruit-in-bowl still life painting above the fireplace mantel. It looked like it might have come from the same furniture store as the sofa and chairs. A couple of bookcases the same shade as the coffee table, an old-world map and another painting I couldn't quite make out, though it looked like it might have mountains as part of the scene, filled up the rest of the room.

Gabe didn't say anything and I wondered if it was because at fifteen he had yet to develop some hospitality skills, if he was shy, or if we had, in fact, interrupted something to do with the blood spatter on his shirt. "I saw two bikes outside; do you have company?"

His eyes shifted to the right. Behind him, a yellow square of light was cast across the floor from what I assumed was the kitchen. "It's okay," he said. "What's up?"

I had become aware of Carla releasing her sphygmomanometer-like grip on my bicep as I was taking in the décor of the living room, but hadn't noticed she'd moved behind Gabe. She moved as if she were in a museum, her hands behind her back, her head tilted slightly upward as she studied the map.

I took a breath. "Gabe, I was wondering if I could ask you a favor." My eyes focused on Carla in the living room as she leaned to look into the kitchen. In the fuzzy foreground Gabe nodded. Carla's eyes went wide and she screamed.

Gabe flinched, started to turn and I reacted. I grabbed his shoulders, swept his feet out from under him and pushed. He hit the floor with a grunt and I pressed my knee into his chest. Carla had only screamed once and I looked to make sure she was okay. She had a hand over her mouth but she wasn't scared.

I followed her gaze and saw another young man about the same age as Gabe run into the living room. His eyes were wide as he looked at me, but what got my attention was the wide gash across his throat and the amount of blood that had spilled down the front of his shirt. "What the hell is going on?" he said.

The kid's esophagus was cut in half—I could see part of it!—how was he able to breathe, let alone speak? I looked down at Gabe and he was smiling, not a psychotic killer smile, but like a little kid who just got his wish after blowing out the candles on his birthday cake.

"It is so awesome that you guys thought he was hurt," he said.

"They did?" the other boy said. "Cool!" Carla and I looked at each other then back at the boy with the slashed throat. "It's fake," he said and pulled at his neck. The gash, a good amount of apparently fake blood and the severed organs came away in his hands and left a clean rectangle of unmutilated skin. "Gabe, who are these people?"

I stood and helped Gabe to his feet. He was still grinning. "This is the guy I told you about," Gabe said looking at his friend. "Ray."

Then Gabe looked at me and said, "That's Tad. We're working on Halloween ideas. We got jobs at the haunted house this year."

"Well Gabe finally got the real job," Tad said. "He's a better make-up artist than Tiffany Knox. She works at a nail salon after school and helps with the school plays. Big deal. She can't do anything as cool as Gabe does."

I nodded, looked at Carla. Her eyes went wide and she mouthed the word, *Wow!*

"Gabe, where are your parents?" I asked.

"Probably still at work," he said. "Working on Dan is my guess."

"*Working on Dan*? What do you mean?"

The boys looked at each other and shrugged. "My dad is the only mortician in town, and mom works for the county," Gabe explained. "She does the death certificates. That's how they met, you know? Just working in the same field sort of." He smiled sheepishly like he knew it was a macabre subject, but also the way of the world. "Mom also does the make-up for open-casket funerals when the family asks."

"Did Dan's family request make-up?" I asked incredulously.

Gabe shook his head. "Dan didn't have any family. That's why I stopped by all the time. His wife left him a long time ago. He told me his brother was killed in Vietnam, though, and his parents both died a few years ago." He looked at the carpet and then back up at me. "I don't think the funeral's going to be open casket anyway," he said quietly.

Couldn't argue with that. I'd seen the pictures. "What about a job?" I asked. Gabe's eyes were on the verge of overflowing as he relived the day he found Dan Tilley's body and no teenager wants to cry in front of their pals. "Gabe? Where did Dan work?"

"Zephyr Auto Sales," he said. "It's a couple blocks past the school."

"That was…different," Carla said as we drove back to Jasper. We'd only stayed a half hour at the Anderson house, but it was October and full-on darkness was the norm after 5pm.

"Very," I said, "but that kid has got talent. I can easily see him doing movie make-up in a few years."

"Well it scared the baboopas out of me."

"Exactly my point. I don't know what a baboopa is, but I was a bit freaked out too. Did you see how happy he was that we thought it was real? Anyway, it explains why he took those pictures of Dan Tilley's body."

"Actually I thought his parents' jobs kind of explained a lot," Carla said.

"I'm just glad Gabe's on board with the yearbooks," I said and pointed at a sign up the street.

Zephyr Auto Sales was a paved lot with a mobile home trailer encased in faded green siding dropped in the middle. Three steps led up to a small wooden deck and the front door. A sign in the window declared the building to be the office and a *We Finance!* banner was stretched along the side. A slew of used vehicles were scattered across the pavement, parked at angles to the street. Balloons of different hues were tied to door handles, hood ornaments or just taped to windshields and bobbed and ducked in the wind. The lot was brilliantly lit by mercury vapor lights every ten feet or so all the way around the perimeter along with a pair of spotlights aimed directly at the office.

Carla and I stepped out of the Land Cruiser and stretched. I walked over to a champagne-colored Subaru, looked in the driver's side window and began counting in my head. One...two...three...four...five...

"Hello, sir," a happy voice behind me said. "That is a beauty of a car right there."

I turned around and looked at the young man who'd taken less than six seconds to come over and try to make a sale. He was in his twenties, had longish blond hair and a thick, rounded beard darker than his hair. He wore black slacks and a bright blue windbreaker over a shirt and tie. "Hi," I said and stuck out my hand. "I'm Ray Gordon."

"Mr. Gordon," he said as he shook my hand, "I'm Mitch. Mitch McCreedy." He handed me a card and I read, *Zephyr Auto Sales, The last place you'll shop for a used car. Mitch McCreedy, Sales Associate.* I squinted at the slogan and wondered if it was a good thing or a bad thing to be the last place to shop. "You've got a good eye, Mr. Gordon," Mitch said. "This Subaru is only a couple of years old, has hardly any mileage on it and is in great shape. In fact—"

I held up my hand. "Sorry, Mitch, but we're not here for a car. I want to ask you about Dan Tilley."

His salesman smile slid away like melted wax. "Oh. Yeah, sure. You a cop or something?"

"Not a cop," I assured him. "Just curious. What did Dan do here?"

"Sales Manager. Well, overall manager, I guess."

"What does that mean?" Carla asked.

"He didn't own the place," Mitch said looking from Carla to me. "That'd be Barbara Devarro. She lives in California, but had Dan run the show."

"You don't sound too happy about that," I said. He shrugged. "Was Dan not a very good manager?"

Mitch looked over his shoulder at the office. No one else was outside. He turned back and said flatly, "Nope."

Carla took a step toward him. "Why not?"

"Honestly, he was kind of an ass. He kept a bottle of whiskey in his desk drawer and had to get a fresh one every few days. He didn't really do anything except order us around. Probably couldn't tell the difference between a Subaru and a Ford."

"Is that what everyone else here thought of him too?"

Mitch nodded. "Nobody here liked him. We were talking this morning about not even going to the funeral. That would be pretty mean and petty though. At least that's what Charlene thinks."

"Charlene another sales person?"

"No, she does the books."

I nodded. "What do you think happened to Dan?"

Mitch's face went pasty white and he shook his head. "I don't know. I've heard rumors, but they seem kind of stupid if you know what I mean."

I nodded. "The werewolf."

"Yeah," Mitch said, "the werewolf. I know it's not true, but I heard there was blood everywhere and his arms were torn off, and...I don't know."

"His arms weren't torn off," Carla told him. "Were they?" she asked me under her breath.

"No, his arms were not torn off."

Mitch glanced at the Washington license plate on the Land Cruiser. "How do you know about the werewolf and whether his arms were torn off or not?"

"We were there. Saw the photos right after the body was discovered," I said. "Do you know anyone who hated Dan enough to kill him?"

The young salesman stuffed his hands in his pants pockets. "I don't know anyone who liked Dan, 'cept maybe Jake, the guy who owns Cedar Lake Lodge. But I don't know anyone who hated him enough to do what I heard."

I looked at Carla and made a face to let her know I was done. "Thanks for your time, Mitch," she said.

He pulled a business card from his pocket and handed it to her. "Sure I can't interest you in this Subaru? It's a beaut!"

Carla smiled and said, "Sorry, Mitch."

26

■ When I woke the next morning I was ready to play, but with Cal gone, there were an uneven number of players left so I had a bye. No chess.

Carla was already awake. I found her curled up on the couch in the front room reading *Werewolves of the Western United States*. Her toes were tucked under Morphy and she had half a cup of coffee on the table beside her.

"Trying to stay awake," I asked, "or go back to sleep?"

"Just trying to wrap my head around all of this. Something seems…off."

I nodded as I poured myself a cup of coffee. I walked over and refilled hers. "Like they're connected somehow?"

"What do you mean?"

"I was thinking about it last night. Tilley and Pederson's murders are connected to the werewolf myth."

"What makes you think so?"

I sat down across from her, took a sip of coffee. "Whoever wrote the Russian notes to Jake and his buddies was obviously here in Jasper when the whole werewolf thing came into being. He—or she—was also well aware of the World Chess Championship. I'm not positive about that, but it just seems too much of a coincidence to not be true.

"Anyway, whatever hatred that person had then for Jake and his band of jocks has festered for more than thirty years. Now, here we are at a chess tournament and people are dying."

"Why now, though? You told me Perry has been hosting this tournament for years."

I pointed at the book in her hands. "The werewolf is back. Whoever killed Dan Tilley hated him; I don't think anyone could mutilate a body like that without a pretty deep-seated dislike. But after all these years, it feels like a cover up. The killer is using the werewolf myth to disguise the murders."

"Disguise them how? Murder is murder, right?"

I shrugged. "Maybe disguise is the wrong word. Deflect might be better. Whoever killed Tilley and Pederson is familiar enough with Cindy Bickerman's death that they're recreating the scene to stir up old feelings and fears. Get people in the werewolf state of mind. Remember what Mitch McCreedy said at the car lot? The werewolf rumor mill is running amok." I nodded. "The killer was here in 1972."

"How are you going to sell that to Chief Blunt?"

"I think he's already on board with it. The hard part is finding out who had it in for Jake's group of friends back then. What could they have done that someone would still kill them for so many years later?"

Carla looked at Morphy. "Do you think…it could be…Perry for some reason?" I shook my head. "But he's been here forever and he's all over the werewolf bit."

"No." I shook my head again. "I just can't see it. He's older than Jake by ten years. He wouldn't have even known him and his friends when they were in high school." But Carla had a point. Perry Whitton was a chess fanatic who would have been aware of Fischer's *till tomorrow* comment to Spassky. Also, it had struck me as odd when he'd asked why I thought the person we were looking for had to have been *impressionable*. Was he being defensive?

I sipped my coffee, sat back, and looked at Carla. Yes, Perry was a lifelong resident of Jasper and whether I liked it or not, he would have been at least aware of Jake and his friends. Who wouldn't have been? In a small town in 1972 there wasn't much to do and high school football was probably on everyone's weekend list. But still… "Nope," I said again. "I just can't see it."

Carla shrugged. "Okay."

There was a knock on the door and Carla looked out the window and waved. "It's Perry."

I stood up. "You know, in horror movies they always cut to the real killer after the other characters are talking about the murders. That's how you know who did it."

"Har har."

I told Morphy to stay and held my finger to my lips, then opened the door. "Hi, Perry. What brings you out so early on our day off?"

"Tom Davis was murdered."

27

■ *"Who* was murdered?" I asked.

I felt Carla come up behind me and Perry took a deep breath. "Tom Davis. He was one of Jake's friends who'd received the Russian note in high school."

"Hold on, Perry. Let us get dressed and we'll talk about it over breakfast." I closed the door and left him on the porch so he wouldn't spy Morphy lazing on the couch.

"Who was he talking about?" Carla asked as she tugged on her jeans.

"Jake mentioned him the other night when we were all at Perry's. One of the high school jocks."

"This is getting scary."

I nodded. "Let's go."

Once we were seated in the lodge dining room we ordered coffee but none of us picked up a menu. "Okay, Perry," I said, "what's happened?"

He shook his head. "Tom Davis was murdered a month ago. After Jake gave us all the names the other night, Bill ran a check on them and found out Tom lived in Portland. A neighbor found him in the garage, sitting in his car with his throat slit."

"This was a month ago?" I asked. Perry nodded. "Why is anyone only hearing of it now?"

Perry shrugged. "The guy moved away when he was what, eighteen? Jake probably lost touch, never saw him again."

"What about the other guy?" I asked. "Jake said one of his pals died years ago, but there's still one more."

"Right. Doug Kincaid. No word on him. Bill hasn't been able to track him down."

Carla set her coffee cup down. "Was there any other *damage* to the body in the car?"

Perry shrugged. "Not sure. Bill didn't say anything."

"Would he have?" I asked.

"With what's going on? Probably."

I nodded. "I think so too."

"Maybe it's not the same killer," Carla suggested.

"Possibly," I agreed, "but my guess is, it is. The timing of it all for one thing."

"But she's right," Perry said. "If the body wasn't all torn up—"

"The killer didn't have to do that there. Portland's a big city; a murder like that could be blamed on lots of things. Here though, they have to use the werewolf for cover."

"This doesn't make any sense," Perry said.

"Did the police have any luck running the backgrounds of our chess players?"

He took a drink and shook his head. "None of them have criminal backgrounds."

"What about players who were here in 1972 and now?"

"Hell, Ray, I know everyone in town. There are only two guys in the tournament who fit that bill. You played one of them already."

"Who?"

"Henry Bagnolde and Leonard Nail."

I shook my head. "Leonard told me he'd retired here only four or five years ago."

"That's right, and he's been telling people that for the past ten years. About four years after he actually did retire he was in a pretty nasty car accident while he was on his way back from a vacation up in Washington. The steering wheel was actually broken where his head hit it. That's what he remembers, retiring four years ago, but he still plays pretty good chess."

"Yes, he does. Okay, how about the other guy, Bagnolde?"

"Henry used to be a jeweler. Nothing big, but he had his own store here for a long time. He was the only game in town so he made out quite well."

"I bet," Carla chimed in.

Perry shrugged. "He wasn't too over the top with his prices, but he must have charged more than necessary. Not too many people can retire ten years early."

"He retired at fifty-five?" Carla asked.

"Yep. And that was fifteen years ago. There's some family money too. His wife's grandfather owned one of the two grocery stores in town."

"It sounds like they're Jasper's royalty," I said.

"I suppose so. Pretty people with money. But they're still here, they're spending their money here and that's good for the community."

"Jasper is important to you, isn't it?" Carla asked.

Perry stared at her, but he looked through her. "I've been here my whole life and I know everyone who lives here. Those people are what makes it important. So yes. Jasper is everything. To me and Della."

"Perry, you said Henry Bagnolde owned a jewelry store. What about Leonard? What did he do before he retired?"

"School teacher. He taught science at the high school."

I thought about that for about five seconds. "Do you know if he had any run-ins with students? Like, maybe, Jake and his buddies?"

"Sure. I don't know about Jake, but most of the students didn't like him. He took his calling as a scientist pretty seriously and high school students, they just couldn't relate."

"*And?*"

"And what? You know teenagers. They were probably worse back then than today, but yeah, they used to pull all kinds of pranks on him."

"I'm almost afraid to ask," Carla said.

Perry leaned on the table. "The worst one was when someone made him drink his frogs."

"Excuse me?" Carla gawked.

"Disgusting, right?"

"Very," Carla agreed and made a Mr. Yuck face. "Tell us about it."

"Leonard was a runner back then, got caught up in the whole Prefontain craze. You know who he was?" I nodded, Carla shook her head. "Steve Prefontain was a, no, *the*, premiere 10,000 meter runner in the country when he went to school at the University of Oregon. He ran in the 1972 Olympics but just missed a medal. It was too bad because everyone, even the guys he ran against, thought he was a phenomenon. He was killed in a car crash not too long after that. Really too bad. Man, he could run.

"Anyway, Leonard, along with the thousands of Oregonians and people all over the U.S. took up running as exercise. Leonard also religiously drank a protein shake every day at lunch. He had a blender in the teacher's lounge, the ingredients in the fridge and so on. He was famous for it.

"So one day he goes to his class and there are three frogs missing from their specimen jars. You see, they were scheduled to dissect frogs that week and they used live ones, made the students kill them and then do the work. In the past though, some of the more, uh, weak-stomached students couldn't handle the *freshness*, if you will. So Leonard kept a few frogs in formaldehyde. Those were easier to work on for those students because the organs were like rubber and it was like working on a model."

Perry shrugged as if to say he just didn't get some people and sipped his coffee. "Do I want to hear the rest of this?" Carla asked.

"I do!" I said.

Perry winked at Carla. "The dissection was the period just after lunch and Leonard had one of those overhead projectors for the instructional diagrams. You know, they had clear sheets of plastic and the teacher could write notes and so forth for the whole class to see. Any way, he turns on the projector and written over the first diagram is, *Did your shake taste a little froggy today?*

"You see, whoever did it had somehow gotten into the teacher's lounge, blended up the three frogs and mixed it in with his stash of ingredients. He spent a week in the hospital."

"From what? Frogitous?" I quipped.

Perry shook his head. "Formaldehyde poisoning."

"Who did it?" I asked.

Perry shrugged. "To this day, at least as far as I know, no one has ever been caught."

"Formaldehyde poisoning," Carla said. "Eww."

"You guys hungry?" Perry asked.

"Not anymore," Carla said.

Our waitress stopped at our table, pen and pad at the ready. "Hey, you guys," she said.

"Nice to see you again," Carla said.

"Good morning, Carey," Perry said. "We were just talking about your dad."

28

■ "Leonard Nail is Carey the Waitress's dad," I mused. "That's interesting."

Carla looked at me from behind her book. "Why is that interesting?"

After breakfast Perry had gone down to the basement to go over details of the final two rounds of the tournament while Carla and I had retreated to our cabin. "I wonder why she didn't mention her father was in the chess tournament. Seems like a rational part of the conversation since she knew I was playing."

Carla shrugged. "Maybe she thought you'd divulge some of your great chess wisdom and then she could report back to him so he could use it against you."

"Somehow I don't think that's it. Do you remember why she came back to Jasper?"

"She said she was homesick."

"Right. I didn't believe it then; even less now. After what Perry told us about Leonard, I think she probably had to come back to take care of him."

"You're probably right, and she doesn't feel good about it either. She didn't want to talk about her dad when Perry told her we'd been discussing him."

"Or, like you said, she was upset that I beat him." I smiled.

Jasper High School was a blocky two-story behemoth of old stone and brick masonry. A wide set of concrete stairs swept up to the three double doors, the many windows around the building had been replaced with modern double-paned glass and the roofline was studded with ramparts and sharp finials that made the school look like a fortress.

I pulled into a *Visitors Only* space, turned off the engine and looked at my watch. "Less than ten minutes." We were there to meet Gabe Anderson at noon in the parking lot of the school. He would bring the yearbooks out after having determined which four covered Jake Humboldt's high school career. The lunch bell would ring at 11:55am; we were there with time to spare and we thought it would only take Gabe about five minutes or less to find Jake in the yearbooks surrounding 1972. I didn't think borrowing library books could be such a challenge, but it turned out that yearbooks were part of the *Special Collections* and not available to check out. In fact, they were not to leave school property. Which is exactly why Gabe had been excited to be in on the scheme to break school rules. The way he looked at it, the parking lot was school property so *he* wouldn't be breaking the rules, but he couldn't stop me from leaving with them.

It was a stretch and he knew it, but 1) I didn't think there could be any serious repercussions, 2) I didn't think anyone would miss a fistful of yearbooks from the early 1970s and 3) if I was wrong about numbers one and two, I would make sure I took all of the heat and Gabe could play dumb.

At 11:55am the Jasper High School lunch hour bell rang. I looked up expecting to see a wave of students breach the front doors of the school in a mad dash to hit the fast food joints downtown. Instead, one of the three sets of doors opened and Gabe Anderson, wearing his signature gray knit cap, came out and scanned the parking lot. He spotted us in the Land Cruiser and trotted over. "I guess we're not in Seattle, huh?" I said to Carla.

She smiled. "I think it would be an insult to call it *quaint*, but the lack of crowds is appealing."

I lowered the window and Gabe swung his backpack off his shoulder as he came over. "Hey, Ray," he said. "Hey, Carla."

"Hey," Carla and I said together.

There was an array of zippers, pockets, snaps and straps on Gabe's backpack that gave it an aura of tactical warfare rather than a bag of school supplies. He selected a zipper and pulled it open. "Here you go," he said and handed me four old Jasper High School yearbooks through the open window. "Mr. Humboldt was a sophomore in 1972 so you got '71 through '74."

"Perfect. Did you have any trouble?" I asked.

He shook his head. "Nah. Nobody looks at them. You should have seen all the dust."

"It would be our luck," Carla said, "if someone decided they wanted to look at them now."

Gabe shrugged. "Don't know why they would. Everyone has their own yearbooks, right?"

"Good point," I said. "Okay, thanks, Gabe. We'll have these back to you in a day or so. In the meantime, if anyone says anything about it, give them my name and have them talk to Chief Blunt at the police station."

He nodded, turned and trotted back to the school.

I started up the Land Cruiser, eased out of the parking lot and turned toward downtown Jasper, which was a block away. "How about we find somewhere else besides Kathy's Café for lunch?" I asked Carla. "We can look through these groovy '70s yearbooks without being bothered by all the cool kids."

Carla squinted at me. "I thought *we* were the cool kids."

I nodded. "Far out."

"What do you have in mind? I don't really want fast food."

"I thought I saw what looked like an Italian place down a side street, but I didn't see the name."

"What made you think it was Italian?"

"It had a red and white striped awning."

"Are you sure it wasn't a barber shop?"

I smiled. "There it is." I pointed to my right, steered off Main Street and pulled to a stop in front of the restaurant.

"*A-Number 1 Mongolian Bar-B-Que,*" Carla read. The sign on the window was red and white foil that matched the awning. "I don't think we're going to get spaghetti and meatballs," Carla said with a smile.

"No, but Mongolian barbeque sounds just fine to me. Shall we?" I got out of the car and opened the passenger door for Carla. "Spicy noodles, senora?"

29

■ We sat near the front window for the light and laid out the four yearbooks. Jasper High School's colors were orange and black and their mascot was an axe-wielding lumberjack. The hard covers of the books alternated in the school colors, 1971 was orange, 1972 was black and so on. The year of the book and *Jasper High School Lumberjacks* was embedded in black lettering on the orange covers and in orange lettering on the black covers. The lumberjack was prominent on each cover as well and struck different poses from year to year. On 1971 the mascot was standing with his booted feet spread, his axe blade on the ground and he held the hilt with his left hand; his right hand held up two fingers in a peace sign and he sported round-framed John Lennon-style specs along with a cheesy grin. 1971: peace, love and a cord of wood.

I opened the 1971 yearbook and quickly thumbed the pages to the freshman class. We needed to see how a young Jake Humboldt and friends looked so we could spot them elsewhere in the book. Carla spotted him first and put her finger on the page. The postage stamp sized black and white photo showed a gawky fourteen-or-so year old with slicked and combed hair — like all of the other boys in the class — and wearing a white shirt and tie. Nothing extraordinary except the tie had a knot as big as my fist.

We looked up the other four boys who'd received the Russian note and then slowly flipped through the entire yearbook in search of their pictures. I wanted to see what clubs they belonged to, what sports they played and any candid shots high school yearbooks are famous for.

It didn't take long. Jasper is a small town and the high school yearbook was less than forty pages. The group of boys all played on the Junior Varsity football and basketball teams and we spotted two of them in random photos of students about the school. Dan was photographed sitting in a hallway reading an English textbook, the caption read, *Freshman Daniel Tilley can't get enough of Mr. Madole's English class*. Gary Lombard was pictured walking down what appeared to be the same hallway with his arms around two girls, a confident smile on his face. The caption read, *High school seems to agree with freshman Gary Lombard*. No doubt the people who wrote those captions went on to be highly respected news reporters of the highest caliber.

That was it for 1971. As freshmen, Jake and his friends kept out of the limelight. At least in terms of yearbook photos.

As I pushed 1971 to the opposite side of the table and took a couple bites of noodles, Carla pulled the black-covered 1972 yearbook forward. She opened it up and we were met with a full-page color portrait of a teenage girl.

Her long straight hair was the color of dead pine needles, and her smile was bored, as if she thought, *Fine, I'll smile if I can leave.* She wore a buttoned to the neck white dress with small purple flowers embroidered around the Peter Pan collar and a purple hairband. She wasn't beautiful, but she wasn't ugly and her eyes sparkled in a way that made me think she might have been up to no good at any given time but no one would ever find out.

At the top of the page in white lettering was *In Memoriam* and below was her name and dates of her birth and untimely death: *Cindy Bickerman, 1957 – 1972.*

"There she is," I said quietly, "the werewolf victim."

I looked out the window and thought about Cindy Bickerman. What happened all those years ago? She wasn't blown up like Otto the moose; according to Dr. Melman there was evidence of post-mortem *discombobulation.* Cindy's body was savagely mutilated *after* she died and the authorities at the time surmised it was to hide the fact that Cindy was murdered, or at least to confuse them about how.

I waved at a car that drove by and Carla turned the page of the yearbook. "Who was that?" she asked.

"Vick. I played him yesterday."

"Aren't you Mr. Popular in Jasper, Oregon? You just know everybody."

"Well, he didn't wave back. But I don't think he saw me, so yes, I am Mr. Popular."

We paged through the yearbook, found the five sophomore portraits and a few other photos featuring the boys. All five were on the varsity football team, but remained JV for basketball. Jake and Dan were both bigger and more muscular than they'd been in their freshman photos. The other three were bigger too, naturally; they were teenage boys, but it looked like Jake and Dan had spent the summer in between the school years lifting weights.

Carla turned a few pages and stopped. "Aww, high school sweethearts," she said. The picture she looked at was of Jake and then Wendy Nelson sitting on the tailgate of a pick-up truck and talking. They were smiling and both wore jackets, jeans and sneakers. It didn't look like they knew they were being photographed. They weren't posed and they weren't looking at the camera. Carla guessed the picture was taken during a lunch hour or maybe at an outdoor pep rally.

There was no mention of Cindy Bickerman other than the dedication at the beginning, and there were no other photos of Jake and his friends.

The 1973 and 1974 yearbooks were even less helpful. The five friends played football throughout high school, but only Jake, Doug and Tom stayed with the basketball team. I had hoped to find some evidence of high school rivalries, maybe a photo with some kid in the background giving Jake the evil eye or some mention of the clubs or groups who competed against one another. But there was nothing obvious, just sports schedules and scores, the annual school play and its list of cast members, the dances and their royalty. For the most part students still dressed in a shirt and tie when they sat for photos. A few wore sweaters and fewer still had the unkempt hair, jeans jackets and fringe-laden vests that marked them as anti-establishment hippies. Jake Humboldt and his friends were self-described jocks and they each had combed hair and ties for their class photos.

The yearbooks were a bust. At least where Jake and his buddies were concerned. We couldn't find any photo that might have led to a suspect. Admittedly, it was a long shot. On the other hand, we did see a portrait of Cindy Bickerman and could finally put a face with the fifteen-year-old victim's name.

30

■ Carla and I kept the yearbooks instead of returning to the high school and risk Gabe getting caught out in the parking lot. He'd told us no one would miss them anyway so we thought it would be just as well to hold on to the books and return them later. It was a small town after all, and we knew where he lived if it really came down to it.

I put the yearbooks in the car and grabbed Carla's hand. "How about a coffee or a piece of pie somewhere?"

"Okay. What's on your mind?"

"What do you mean?"

"You haven't said anything for a while and now you want to walk. You're thinking about something."

"Fair enough," I said and steered her toward Main Street. "I'm thinking about the argument Jake and Wendy had the other night. Carey said the lodge isn't a continual money maker and they might be in trouble financially. I thought maybe Dan Tilley was a silent partner or something but that wasn't the case. Whatever their argument was about, we know Jake did something Wendy had asked him not to do."

"Right. What made you think about that?"

"The picture of them when they were younger. Like you said, they were high school sweethearts. Now they're married and still living in Jasper. They've seen it all."

"So?"

"So I'm having a tough time believing they've been here their whole lives and acted so shocked when we believed someone is after him and his little band of buddies."

"You think they did something?"

I shrugged. "Maybe, maybe not. It seems to me we have a number of people who have motive. I just don't know if all those people have it in them to kill, or even if their motives are powerful enough to drive them to it."

We went into the Jasper Java Pit and ordered espressos. "Which people are you talking about?" Carla asked as we sat down at a small table.

I leaned over and spoke quietly. Everyone knows everyone in small towns and I didn't want any rumors or overheard comments to make it further than the door. "Jake and Wendy Humboldt."

"Motive?" Carla whispered.

"Finances of some sort," I said and Carla nodded. "Dr. Thuringer. Book sales." She squinted. "It's weak, but it's a possible motive, as is his wanting to look more like an expert, so we'll change it to sales and ego. Carey Nail—"

"What? Where did *that* come from?"

"I know, but think about it. Everything Perry told us about how kids would pull pranks on her father, how he ended up in the hospital, and then how she clammed up when he told her we were talking about Leonard. What if she thinks Jake, Dan and the others had done something to her dad? What if they were the ones who put him in the hospital all those years ago and his memory problems are because of formaldehyde poisoning and not the car accident?"

Carla shook her head slowly and sipped her espresso. "I don't know, Ray."

"It's a stretch, but it's a possibility. I'm just trying to put everything on the table."

"What about Perry?"

I nodded reluctantly. "He's been here his whole life and he's desperate to see Jasper thrive. Murder tourism seems far-fetched, but you're right, it's also plausible."

"How about Dan's co-workers?"

"The salesman we talked to, Mitch, wasn't old enough to be around in 1972," I said.

"Right, but we didn't talk to anyone else. Maybe one of the others had more of a motive than just not liking their boss."

"Again, it's possible," I said, "but I didn't get that feeling. Besides, Chief Blunt has never mentioned the car lot or Dan's former co-workers. I don't think he or his officers are inept enough to not have questioned them."

Carla nodded. "Is that it then?"

"There's still the chance one of the chess players could be involved. Perry said the police didn't find anything…"

"But?"

"But the police only did a background check. They put the names into the system and nothing came up. That only means none of the players have been arrested before; it doesn't mean they're all innocent. There are plenty of criminals out there without a record. They just haven't been caught yet."

"That's comforting. Can they look deeper into someone's background?"

"Yes and no. Blunt probably won't dig any deeper with the chess players. Without any suspicion on any of them and no records to speak of, why would he?" I shrugged. "Can't blame him. Maybe he'll find something on Thuringer. As long as he says it correctly."

Carla smiled and raised her eyebrows. "What are you going to do?"

"Why Miss Caplicki, whatever do you mean?"

"Oh I know you're not going to let this go. I'd be disappointed if you did."

I smiled. "I think we should invite Carey over again or take her to dinner. I want to get her talking about Leonard, see if her story lines up with Perry's."

"What if it does?"

"Then that's that. And then we see if she'll look into the books of Cedar Lake Lodge."

"Do you have ulterior motives for every suspect you question?"

"It's nice to have options." *Options*. For some reason that word resonated like a house of mirrors and pulled an image across my mind.

"What are you thinking?" Carla asked.

"Hold on one second." I pulled my phone out of my pocket and dialed. Hopefully Perry wasn't still out at the lodge where there was no cell service. He picked up on the second ring.

"Hi, Ray. What can I do for you?"

"Perry, do you know Vick Tomlinson?"

"Not personally. He's never played here before. At least not that I remember."

"Do you know where he's from?"

"Oregon. Over on the coast I think. You and Ryan Brooks are the only players from out of state."

"Okay, thanks. I'll catch up with you later."

"What's wrong?" Carla asked.

I tucked my phone back into my jacket pocket. "Remember the guy I waved to just a bit ago? Vick? Perry says he's from the Oregon coast."

"So?"

"So the car he was driving had Idaho plates."

31

 "Idaho license plates don't necessarily mean he's not from Oregon," Carla said a bit too haughtily. "Maybe it's a rental."

"Of course, but it's something that needs to be checked out. I'm sure Chief Blunt will be happy to hear from us again."

"Us? He's never yelled at me."

"He won't yell at you either. You're very easy on the eyes."

"Sexist, but I'll take it."

I winked and smiled at her. "Facts are facts."

The police station was quiet. No citizens were lodging complaints against their neighbors, no elementary students were there on a field trip and the officer on desk duty welcomed us with the same kind of smile we'd been met with at the car lot.

"We'd like to see Chief Blunt," I told him.

"Can I get your name?"

"Ray Gordon."

"Oh." His smile collapsed like an imploded building. "Well, uh, Chief Blunt isn't available at the moment. Can I take a message?"

"I've been blacklisted, huh?" The officer's face was stony. "Fine," I said. He handed me a pen and pad and I wrote, *Vick Tomlinson, chess player in the tournament, says he's from OR, drives car with ID plates.* I looked at Carla and added, *Probably nothing, maybe a rental, but you never know.*

I tore off the paper and handed it back to the desk sergeant and he put it in a file folder. "Okay," he said, "I'll get it to him."

I wasn't sure why I was suddenly on Chief Bill Blunt's bad list, though I suspected it was because none of the chess players had stirred up any leads. I had insisted the police start with them and he likely thought I'd wasted his time. Well, not *his* time, but the department's in general.

"What now?" Carla asked. We were outside the police station and I stopped at the bottom of the stairs. I had asked myself the same question when we walked out the door.

I took her hand in mine and led her to the car. "Now we go back to the cabin. Morphy is probably in dire need of a fire hydrant and I need to prepare for tomorrow's game. We'll stop at the lodge first, though, and see if Carey is available later."

"Are you going to accuse her of murder?"

"No. Not directly anyway." I smiled.

"Do you think the police will follow up on the license plate thing?"

I thought about it for a minute. If I was right and Blunt believed I'd wasted man-hours to do background checks on a handful of chess players, would he bother to look into a car from Idaho being driven by a man from Oregon? "No," I said.

Carla stopped at the side of the Land Cruiser. "But it's going to gnaw on you isn't it?"

"Yes."

"Is, what's his name, Vick, still in the tournament, or did you knock him out?"

"I think he's still in it. It's double elimination and I think I handed him his first loss."

"So let's find his car tomorrow and get the plate number. We can get the name the car's registered under and put your mind at ease."

I nodded and kissed her. "Good idea." I opened the passenger door and Carla climbed in.

32

■ At 9pm Carey Nail walked through the door of Eli's, a small pub where Jasper locals hung out and enjoyed a drink or two away from the more touristy spots. When we'd stopped and invited her over for a drink, Carey had suggested we meet at Eli's after her shift. She wore jeans and a mid-length raincoat the color of an old nickel. Carey's hands were in her pockets and she turned her head slowly as she scanned the place.

Carla waved from where we were throwing darts at a well-worn board whose number twenty segment looked like Omaha Beach on D-Day and Carey made her way over. "Wanna throw a few?" I asked her.

"No thanks. I'm more of a horseshoes type."

"Really?"

She smiled. "No, not really. What are we drinking?"

"Beer okay?" Carla asked. Carey nodded and I went to the bar.

When I returned they were sitting in a booth and two men had taken over the dartboard. Carey had taken off her coat and I noticed, as I'm sure all of the other men in the bar did too, that it wasn't just her waitress uniform which was tight. She wore a purple blouse with the top three buttons open, and I was pretty sure it was because they *couldn't* be buttoned. I placed the beers on the table and slid in next to Carla.

"Thanks for inviting me," Carey said. "I don't really go out very often."

Carla and I glanced at each other and I felt a pang of guilt. Did I really need to ask Carey a bunch of questions about a murder case? It wasn't even *my* case; I was a chess teacher, not a detective. Did it even matter?

"Oh," Carey said. "You want to talk about something."

Busted. "Nothing bad," I said, but I could practically feel Carla's gaze. "You just got my curiosity stirred up."

"About my dad?"

I nodded. "Why didn't you tell me before that he was in the chess tournament?"

Carey shrugged and drank some beer. "Would you believe me if I told you I was hoping to get some chess secrets out of you?"

"Ha!" Carla said and she slapped the table. "That's what I told him!"

I shook my head. "But that's not the reason."

Carey gulped down half the beer in the glass and then stared at me for a moment. "Okay. What I said about coming back here because I was homesick was a lie. I had to come back to take care of him, and frankly, I was pissed about it. I had a good job in Portland and I loved it there. But his memory just got worse and worse, then Mom died and there's only me. His teacher's salary wasn't enough to pay for in-home care so I came back to Jasper. I wasn't happy about it and that made me feel like shit too. I mean, what kind of daughter am I if I was upset about taking care of my own father when he needed me?"

"Normal, I expect," I said.

"So you know?"

I shook my head. "Unfortunately, I don't. My parents were killed when I was eleven."

"Oh, me and my big mouth. I'm sorry."

"Don't worry about it." For some reason people always felt like they'd hurt me when I told them I was an orphan. I'm sure it was because they thought they had suddenly reminded me I'd grown up without parents, as if I'd somehow forgotten. "I'm the one who should apologize to you," I said. "I didn't mean to make you feel guilty."

"You didn't," Carey said. She finished her beer. "I always feel that way."

Carla gave Carey's hand a squeeze. "Don't feel bad about a little resentment. You're here aren't you? It's not like you said no and abandoned him."

"I suppose."

I took a couple swallows of beer and gave them a moment. I watched the two guys who had taken over the dartboard. They were landing enough triple twenties to make me figure they spent a lot of time at Eli's. There were two pool tables toward the back, a couple of older-looking pinball machines and the rest of the space was taken up with tables and the long mahogany bar where a lot of people were perched and watching football on a couple of flat screen TVs that hung from the ceiling.

Carey had teared up a little and was dabbing at her eyes. "So we heard your dad was quite the teacher," I said. Carla looked at me as she recognized my not-so-subtle attempt to steer the conversation away from the gloomy duties of progeny and towards the much darker depths of motives for murder. Carey didn't seem to mind though.

"Yep. Mr. Nail, high school biology, years one through four, assistant football coach and basketball season concession stand manager."

"Did you have to take his classes?" Carla asked.

"Sure. Everyone had to take at least one year of biology."

"Was he popular?" I asked. "Perry told us some students played some pretty harsh pranks."

Carey shrugged. "He was disappointed sometimes but he took it in stride. He figured they wouldn't do it if they didn't like him. I don't remember any of the pranks being *harsh* though."

Carla and I looked at each other. Was she thinking the same thing I was, that it was a red flag that Carey seemed to not remember her father spending a week in the hospital after drinking a concoction of blended frogs?

"Oh," I said, "well, Perry told us your dad got formaldehyde poisoning once and was pretty sick for a while."

"Oh, *that*." Carey nodded. "That was pretty bad. I'd forgotten about the frogs."

"Do you have any idea who did it? Perry said they were never caught."

"I don't know who it was, but Dad does. There were three of them and they came and visited him in the hospital. He said they cried the whole time they were in his room."

"Who were they?" Carla asked.

Carey shrugged again. "Dad refused to have them punished. He said they admitted it, they were sorry and he accepted their apologies. Never even said if they were boys or girls."

Mr. Nail, Jasper High School Biology teacher, exercise nut and imbiber of liquefied frogs had forgiven his tormentors and Carey wasn't exactly incensed over her father's past pranksters either. I looked at Carla, shook my head and mentally scratched Carey from the list of suspects. It wasn't really a surprise given how weak her motive was — at least from my point of view — but an outside chance is still a chance and lives can change on just a chance.

The waitress stopped at our table and I ordered another round. We made small talk until the waitress returned with our beers and then I said, "Carey, the real reason I wanted to talk to you tonight was to ask a favor."

"Oh? It wasn't to discuss my dad?" She smiled.

"This might get you into a little trouble, but would you be willing to somehow look into the financial situation of Cedar Lake Lodge? Specifically their accounting records?"

She looked from me to Carla and back again. "Why? I thought someone was going after Jake and his high school friends? That's what Wendy told me."

I nodded. "It definitely seems to be the case. But remember the argument we all heard, the one you came and talked to us about?"

She nodded. "Of course."

"Something about it just strikes me as odd."

"What? You think Jake and Wendy are somehow getting money for Dan's death?"

I shrugged. "I really don't know. Possibly. It just seems strange that they were arguing pretty heavily about something Wendy specifically asked Jake not to do and he apparently did anyway, and that was right after Dan Tilley's murder. Are they connected? Maybe, maybe not. I'm just trying to cover all the squares."

"You mean bases?" Carey asked.

Carla laughed and shook her head. "No, he means squares, as in the squares of a chessboard."

Carey stared at me. "Well, like I told you before," she said, "I won't do anything to get Jake and Wendy in hot water, but I can tell you this: Cedar Lake Lodge is in serious trouble financially. They're going to put it up for sale as soon as the tournament is over."

"How do you know it's financial? Maybe they just want out of the business," I said.

Carey shook her head. "Nope. Wendy let me know before I left after my shift. She said they can't afford it anymore, they can't afford the help, the upkeep, any of it. Everybody is gone as soon as the tournament is over."

Carla put her hand over Carey's again. "What about you?"

"I got laid off tonight. I'm already out of a job."

33

■ The next round of the chess tournament was scheduled to begin at 10am and there was a lot to think about. I'd never been undefeated this far into a tournament and it made me feel like there was a train rushing toward me while I walked the tracks without a care. It was exhilarating, but I knew I had to be careful.

The night before, after Carey had left Eli's, Carla and I went back to the cabin and discussed her idea about Vick Tomlinson's license plate. There wasn't much to the plan: wait until he arrived at the lodge for the tournament and write down his plate number. Carla would then go into town to see if anyone at the courthouse could help her attach a name to the registration. Simple.

After breakfast in the lodge dining room I went downstairs and left Carla to her own devices. She had a view of the stairway leading down to the tournament room and would drink coffee until she saw Vick. Once the round started at 10am she would be free and clear.

I sat down at board one and adjusted my pieces. I was playing white against Alan Kirkpatrick. Perry told me Alan was from Eugene and taught Medieval Literature. I checked my watch. 9:50am. My opponent stood by the pairing sheets and drank coffee. He *looked* like a lit prof with his navy corduroys and elbow-patched tweed sports coat. All he needed was a beat up leather book bag and a pipe to really sell it.

Vick Tomlinson was nowhere in sight, but his opponent, Don Fitzgerald, was sitting at board two staring at me. I nodded at him and went back to centering my pieces in their squares. I liked my pieces to be uniform before the game started. It's not like I pulled out a ruler and got them exact, I just liked them in the middle so the ranks were neat. More than anything it helped me focus on the board, push away the world around me.

Perry stood up and moved out from behind his table. Fitzgerald continued to stare at me so I stared back and pushed the tip of my nose up. He shook his head and turned to look up the stairs. *Ha!* I won.

Perry checked his watch, glanced toward the staircase and then at me. I pointed to board two as if I wasn't sure who he was looking for. He nodded and I shrugged. I didn't know where Vick was and I suddenly wondered if Carla was okay. There was no reason for her to be in danger; we hadn't told anyone except the Chief of Police about Vick's license plate and besides, it was just a license plate.

I checked my watch. 9:58am. If Vick didn't show up the match would start anyway. Perry would start the clock on board two and Vick would either show up and play or lose when his time ran out.

It was then, just as Perry was about to announce the start of the round that Vick Tomlinson pounded down the staircase like an overgrown teenage boy late for a first date. His face was flushed and his right pant leg was bunched up under his knee. "Flat tire," he huffed. "Sorry."

Vick sat in his seat at board two, Alan sat down across from me and Perry said, "You may start your clocks."

I brought my pawn to the e4 square to begin the game. The night before I'd decided to play a common opening, the Ruy Lopez, which every budding chess player learns, and then see what defense my opponent would attempt.

Alan responded by bringing his pawn to e5 which told me nothing. I moved my Knight to f3 to attack his pawn and he protected it with Nc6. Alan moved quickly, like he'd played the *Ruy Lopez* since childhood — which he probably had — so I decided to change it up. I moved the pawn in front of my Queen to the d4 square instead of my Bishop to b5. This was the opening for the Scotch and it could lead to strange positions.

BLACK

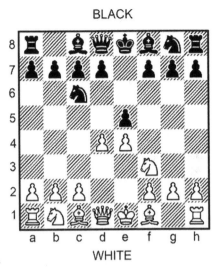

WHITE

Scotch Opening after 3. d4

If I wasn't prepared to be a bit creative, the Scotch could be difficult. On the other hand, I didn't want to make Alan's game very comfortable either. I looked at the carved mane of my Knight and thought. Vick said he was late because of a flat tire. Was he late because he fixed it or because he had to get a ride as his car was now in a shop having the tire repaired? What was with the pant leg? After a minute ran off Alan's clock, he captured my d4 pawn with his own pawn on e5.

Carla appeared in the stairwell and sat down on a step when she caught my eye. She pointed at Vick Tomlinson's back and then mimed riding a bicycle. I nodded, captured Alan's pawn on d4 by replacing it with my Knight and stopped my clock.

Vick Tomlinson rode a bicycle around the lake in order to get to the tournament on time.

34

■ "Why would Vick ride a bicycle?" I asked Carla. "It's too cold in the mornings isn't it? If he's staying in town, that's a long ride around the lake."

Carla shook her head and slurped her soup. It was just past two in the afternoon and we were enjoying hot soup and sandwiches at Kathy's Café following my win over Alan Kirkpatrick. "Wendy said there were a few who registered late for the tournament and the lodge was already full by then. I thought Carey the waitress told us business was tough. Weird, don't you think?"

"Yes, but she also said the chess tournament was one of the few times they were full. I don't suppose Wendy knows where he *is* staying?"

"Nope. It's a small town though. Can't be too many hotels."

I shrugged. "Maybe it's not worth it."

Carla stopped her spoon just above the bowl. "What happened to checking every possibility?"

She was right of course, but somewhere along the way I began to think an out of state license plate wasn't a clue, but rather a tangent down the wrong path. It was true that I initially believed one of the chess players was more than likely involved in Dan Tilley's and Cal Pederson's murders, but anybody who'd been caught up in the Fischer mania surrounding the 1972 World Chess Championship—and that was a lot of people—could have written the cryptic Russian note to Jake and the others. "I'm kind of surprised I haven't heard from Chief Blunt," I said. "Usually the police would tell someone like me to butt out of official police business."

"You're not really interfering though," Carla said. "You're making educated suggestions."

"*Educated suggestions.* I like the sound of that. Maybe I should have business cards printed up with that slogan."

"Are you making fun of me, Mr. Gordon?"

"Not at all." I took a bite of my sandwich to keep from smiling.

"You haven't answered the question though. What about Vick Tomlinson and the mysterious license plate?"

"You make it sound like a *Scooby-Doo* episode. I wish this was a cartoon caper; at least no one would be dead." I sighed. "You're right; we still need to check it out. Let's stop by the police station first and see if they've already done it."

Since the Jasper Police Station was on a side street a block off Main, it wasn't exactly a bastion of activity. I imagined a busy night for the local cops (besides the two recent murders) was to park outside Eli's and give the eye to anyone who stumbled toward their car. Jasper was a nice town, though. Like Carla had said, the lack of crowds was certainly appealing, and the residents seemed happy enough with what Jasper had to offer them.

Carla and I went inside the police station and were once again greeted with a silence any library would be happy to acquire. This time a young cop I recognized as one of those who'd come out to the lodge the evening of Cal Pederson's death was watching the front desk. Her uniform had been pressed and had sharp creases down the length of the sleeves, something I hadn't noticed on any of the other officers I'd come across. Her black hair was cut short and she stood motionless, tracking us with her eyes like a creepy painting in a haunted house.

I gripped Carla's elbow and steered her toward the bulletin board. "What?" she whispered. I pulled her along and pointed at some of the flyers on the wall but didn't say anything. I glanced over my shoulder and saw the cop, still facing forward, her eyes canted toward us.

"I'm messing with our silent hostess," I whispered.

Carla looked toward the desk then ducked her chin. "Ray, they already don't like you."

"That hurts." I turned us back the way we came in. "I don't think it's dislike as much as it's..."

"Can I help you two?" the desk cop finally asked.

"Just checking out the literature you have here," I said.

"Not exactly a library."

"Is Chief Blunt available?" Carla asked.

The woman shook her head. "He's out."

"Did he leave any messages for Ray Gordon?" I asked. "That's me."

Her body moved for the first time as she turned to check the counter behind her. There were several trays with names on them. I followed her gaze to the one marked BLUNT. She turned back around to face us. "No."

"Thanks for your help," I said as Carla and I turned and went out.

Carla stopped on the sidewalk and pulled her collar up against the fall wind. "I don't think she likes desk duty."

"Maybe she did something to piss off her boss, got assigned the desk and now she's taking it out on the local denizens."

Carla laughed. "*Denizens*? My, what a big vocabulary you have; it's very archaic."

I bounced up and down on my toes. "Not too weird a word?"

"I'll need to sleep on it. I think you're right about one thing, though. It's weird that Chief Blunt suddenly won't see you anymore."

I shrugged. "Maybe he's really not in. He might be investigating Thuringer; he seemed to like the ego theory. But he wouldn't need to go to another town to do it. A couple of phone calls are all it would take."

"I think it's going to rain," Carla said.

I followed her gaze skyward and took in the dark clouds. When I looked back down I spotted Vick Tomlinson. He rode his bike past the police station and headed west. "Look," I said to Carla and nodded in Tomlinson's direction.

She saw him and said, "What are you going to do?"

"Feel like a walk?"

35

■ Carla and I walked west on Bronze Street. Vick
Tomlinson was about a block and a half ahead of us and
had slowed down. I watched as he looked over his
shoulder and then veered across the street to the Blue
Bucket Motor Inn. A rusted white pole held a sign high
above the street that depicted a big blue bucket tipped at a
forty-five degree angle. Three neon tubes sputtered
weakly to create the effect of water pouring into a painted
likeness of Cedar Lake.

"Blue Bucket?" Carla said. "What's that supposed
to mean?"

I shrugged. "Maybe back in the 1940s, which is
when that sign looks like it was made, they had a view of
the lake."

"Seriously?"

I laughed. "Who knows? Maybe the owner has a
thing for blue buckets. Or the sign company gave him a

deal to get rid of it."

We got closer and saw the Blue Bucket Motor Inn in its full glory. Two long single-story buildings made an L with the office joining the two where they met. The roof was in need of new shingles, the doors were thick with many coats of sand-colored paint and the peeling white-washed walls were undoubtedly a sore point for the city council. I spotted the bicycle Vick had ridden when he'd gone by. It was a racer-orange mountain bike that had seen plenty of muddy trails. "Hey," I said to Carla and nodded toward where the bike stood against one of the posts that held up the overhanging roof like an old west movie set.

"No car," Carla observed.

"Maybe around back."

We continued up Bronze Street until we were just beyond the motel. We were on the edge of town and a small forest of pines and conifers stood about thirty yards from the back of the low buildings, which gave the guests a year-round view of green needles, squirrels and probably more than a few deer. Between the Blue Bucket and the trees was a thin field full of weeds, scrappy grasses and littered with forlorn rusted farm equipment, broken, warped pieces of plywood and nondescript pieces of metal. No cars.

"Must be in the shop," I said.

"Which shop?" Carla asked.

"Like you said with the hotels, it's a small town; there can't be many."

In fact, there were five auto service shops in Jasper. At least one, maybe two more than a town of 3,500 people needed, but one of them worked exclusively on farm vehicles. If Vick's car was in one of those shops, my guess was it would be either the closest one to the Blue

Bucket Motor Inn, or the one closest to Cedar Lake Lodge. Usually a flat tire was discovered before the trip began, or after it had already started and it if it was the latter, Vick would have made the drive through town before feeling the effect of a flat tire.

It started to rain as we backtracked to the Land Cruiser and we ran the last fifty yards. Didn't do any good, we got wet anyway. We drove to Al's Auto Repair, which looked like at one time it had also been a gas station, but though the concrete islands remained, the pumps were gone. The building was white with orange trim and the two bay doors were rolled up. We looked inside but the only car being worked on was a blue Toyota. The parking lot was empty so all of Al's customers, other than the owner of the Toyota, had picked up their cars.

Next was JD's Tires, Shocks & Brakes. *If you're flat, ridin' rough or just can't stop, JD's has you covered.* It was a long gray building with four bay doors, only one of which was open. Warm yellow light spilled through the windows into the ever-darkening, wet afternoon and we saw several employees working below cars on hydraulic lifts. I scanned the parking lot and saw the car Vick Tomlinson had been driving. It was a silver Honda and indistinguishable from a rental or a privately owned vehicle. "There it is," I said and pointed.

"Yep," Carla said, "Idaho plates."

I handed her my cell phone. "I'll drive through the parking lot, you get a picture. Get the whole car so we can get the make and model, but make sure we can read the plate number."

She took the phone and got the camera app ready. I turned into JD's Tires, Shocks & Brakes, drove slow enough to give Carla the time to snap a couple of photos and looked into the open bay door as if searching for a lost dog. One of the mechanics looked out from beneath his car and nodded. I nodded back and raised my hand off the steering wheel in a casual wave.

"Got it," Carla reported as I turned back out onto the street. I turned toward downtown and stepped on the gas. "Now what?"

The first thought I had wasn't a *what*, but a *who*. Tommy Ryder had already been able to get me information I'd asked him for. Why not again, even if I was going to owe him big? "Tommy Ryder comes from a family of cops, remember?" I asked. "I'll send him the photos and see if they can get us the name. I'm sure they can do it faster than us."

"What about John Keller?"

I steered into a diagonal parking slot in front of a cupcake shop and killed the engine. The rain had picked up strength and machine gunned off the roof of the car. "What about him?" I asked.

John Keller had been my partner during my short experience with the Seattle Police Department. We didn't part friends and when I saw him again years later he arrested me for a murder I did not commit in order to make himself look good. It certainly wasn't a moment of male bonding for us. I looked at Carla as if she'd lost her mind. After all, she had been my one phone call from jail, she knew.

"He can probably look it up while you're on the phone with him. Much faster than asking Tommy who's just a middleman. Tell John he owes you for locking you up."

She made a good point, but asking John Keller for a favor was like eating raw liver. Just the idea of it made me sick.

"Ray?"

"Fine." I Googled the precinct in Seattle where Keller was a detective — although for his miserable investigative skills I thought he should have been made a Keystone Kop. I tapped in the number and asked for Detective John Keller.

"Keller. Homicide."

I smiled and thought of Morphy taking a crap on my former partner's front lawn. "Hi, John. It's Ray Gordon." Silence. "Hello?"

"What do you want, Gordon?"

I looked at Carla and she shrugged. "John, I was wondering if I could ask a favor."

He sighed. "I can't wait to hear this."

"I need a name for an Idaho plate number."

"No. You know I can't do that."

"Come on, John. You owe me one."

"What? I *owe* you? For what?"

"Arresting me to make it look like you knew…"

Carla patted my arm and I looked at her. "Go easy," she whispered.

I took a deep breath. "For arresting me when you shouldn't have. How's that?" Silence again. Was he thinking about it? "John?"

"Fine," he said. "Give me the plate. And then we're through. Understand?"

I nodded but didn't say anything and then read him the number. "It's a Honda Civic," I said. "And it's Idaho."

"Yeah, yeah. I got it the first time. Wait one."

Instead of hold music the Seattle Police Department opted for anti-criminal messaging. A therapeutic female voice urged me to buckle up (it's the law!), to not drive under the influence (of anything), and to consider those around me when driving (road rage is bad). Fine points but I thought the police department marketing team should have squad specific communications. For example, I called homicide; instead of traffic issues the recording should tell listeners that kitchen knives are only appropriate for slicing food items, handguns are to be used only for licensed and approved gun range targets and self-defense (though they'd probably leave that out), and finally, over-the-counter poisons were to be used solely for the particular rodent, insect or other unwanted multi-legged creatures specified on the label. Narrow-focus marketing just made sense.

"Gordon?" John spat into the phone.

"Yes, John, I'm here."

"The plate is registered to Peter Mitchell, Boise, Idaho. Got it?"

"Peter Mitchell. Thanks, John."

"You didn't hear it from me. And we're even."

The phone went silent and I shook my head. "What an ass."

"Well, you never were friends," Carla said. "But now we know right? Peter Mitchell owns the car and not Vick Tomlinson?"

I nodded. What was the implication? Probably nothing. More than likely Vick borrowed a friend's car. I looked at Carla. "Would you loan your car to a friend for a whole week?"

She looked out the window as she thought about it. "Depends. Is it my only car?"

"Exactly. A week is a long time to be without transportation. We have to assume this Peter Mitchell has a job and needs to buy groceries."

"Or he's married and his wife has a car too."

I nodded. "Here's the problem: Peter Mitchell and his car live in Boise. Vick Tomlinson says he's from the Oregon coast. That's a long way to drive to lend someone your car."

Carla sat up in her seat, her eyes wide and said, "How about this. Peter is going on vacation, flying international. There's a cheaper flight to wherever he's going out of Portland. Vick needs a car, so Peter drives to Vick's, Vick takes Peter to the airport and then drives here. When Peter gets back all tan and relaxed, Vick will pick him up, Peter will take Vick home, and then Peter will drive for a day back to Boise."

I stared at Carla. "If I was Peter I would give Vick two hundred dollars to rent a car instead of me driving across Oregon, twice, so he could borrow mine."

Carla crossed her arms. "Well you're not considering the power of the Civic." She smiled.

"Or," I thought out loud, "Peter is dead too and Vick stole the car."

"That's morbid," she said, "but the way things are going around here…"

"One way to find out. Let's call Peter."

I tapped Peter Mitchell, Boise, ID into the Google app on my phone and let the search engine do its thing. There was a young man with pictures of himself splashed everywhere the Internet had the ability to post a photo, but he wasn't our man. The photos of young Peter included him on a soccer field, waving from in front of the Disneyland castle, and enough selfies to make any reality TV personality envious. But he looked to be around nine to twelve years old, too young to drive a car. The Peter Mitchell we wanted proved too elusive even for the mighty Internet. There were a few sites that offered to reveal the contact information for every Peter Mitchell in the United States and even their criminal records, for a fee, but I wasn't shopping.

"I got this," Carla said.

She pulled her own phone from her jacket pocket and did a quick Internet search. "What are you looking up?" I asked.

"You'll see. Prepare to be amazed." She found what she wanted, made the telephone connection and with a flick of her head to sweep her hair out of the way, put the phone to her ear.

I noticed the windows were steamed up so I started the engine and turned on the defroster. After a moment Carla said, "Hi, I'm calling from the King County Courthouse in Seattle. If possible I need a phone number and address for a Mr. Peter Mitchell in Boise. Yes, I'll hold." She opened the console between our seats and fished out a napkin. I pulled a pen out of the open storage bay behind the shifter and handed it to her. "Hi, yes," she said into the phone. She wrote what looked like three addresses on the napkin. "Got it. Thank you." She listened again and said, "Oh, we're trying to match the address with a name and license plate number... Yes, it's part of an investigation, but we're not sure if Mr. Mitchell is involved at this point... Okay, yes, if you think they might have more information. Thank you."

I looked at her and she said, "Transferring me to the Clerk's Office." I nodded and then she was speaking into the phone again. "Hi, yes, Peter Mitchell... Actually anything you can provide might be helpful." Carla looked at me and I gave her a thumbs up. "Oh really?" she said into the phone. "What year?" She scribbled on the napkin again and it tore. "Okay, in person. I understand. Thank you so much, you've been a big help."

Carla pocketed her phone and dangled the torn napkin between her finger and thumb. "Well, well, well, *this* is interesting."

"I'm listening," I said. "What was that all about?"

"There happen to be three Peter Mitchells in Boise. One is in a convalescent home, one is the kid all over social media and the third has some sort of history." She smiled but didn't say anything more.

"Go on," I said. "You have my attention."

"The third Peter Mitchell has a sealed file from when he was a boy. 1973 actually." She raised her eyebrows.

"1973, just after the mess here in Jasper." I thought for a minute, but there wasn't any connection. "I assume when you said *in person* it meant they wouldn't tell you over the phone why the file was sealed."

"Right. Only in person. What do you think? Should I go to Boise tomorrow while you're winning the final match?"

"It's probably nothing. The chance of Peter Mitchell being involved is remote at best."

"But Vick has his car and he's here. That makes him involved doesn't it?"

Carla had a valid point. Again. In my gut I felt the owner of the car was probably dead or perhaps Vick had bought the car and not changed the registration yet. Unlikely, but possible. Either way, the murderer was in Jasper at the moment, not Boise. "If you want to check it out," I said, "why not?"

Carla smiled. "Maybe I'll see if Debbie in cabin five wants to go. We'll take Morphy and Sydney for a quick road trip."

"Promise me you'll only go to the courthouse, okay? Don't go to his house. Just get the info and come back."

She nodded and gave me a salute. "Roger that."

36

■ Debbie wanted to visit a bait and tackle shop she'd heard about and gave up a day of fishing for the chance. She and Carla had the dogs secured in the back of the Land Cruiser by 7:30am and were on the road soon after. They would gas up and get breakfast to go. It was a five-hour drive to Boise and Carla didn't expect they'd be at the courthouse very long. "Probably be back in time for dinner," she'd said. "Unless Debbie spends hours shopping for fishing lures."

I showered after they left and took advantage of the quiet cabin to study more tactical chess puzzles. I felt a little guilty preparing for a chess game when there was someone out there wanting to kill Jake Humboldt. It was like eating a piece of pie while watching the kitchen it was baked in go up in flames. On one hand I was here to play chess; on the other hand there was a murderer nearby and, at least in my mind, I might be able to do something about it. Did I play chess or did I stick my nose in someone else's business?

It was disconcerting to think about the murders and the small town of Jasper's trouble while I muddled through chess diagrams and tried to discover a hidden checkmate in four moves. Which is what the murder case was, a puzzle where the next moves needed to be discovered before they were played out. Diagrams were fine, but when playing an entire game it helped to be present from the beginning. The early strategy of an opponent and the moves played out could help determine where the game was headed. In the case of Dan Tilley's and Cal Pederson's murders there were very few clues as to what led up to them.

And then I had my answer. I'd come too far in both the tournament *and* the murder investigation to quit either one. I just needed to focus on them one at a time.

I moved over to the couch, picked up Carla's copy of *Werewolves of the Western United States* and scanned the basic facts of Cindy Bickerman's death. I had just been thinking about the early moves of a chess game and how they rippled out to determine the outcome. The same thing was playing out now but this time lives were at stake and the events of 1972 were determining the outcome of who lived and who died. There was something about Cindy Bickerman's death that somehow connected — aside from the werewolf myth — the murders during the tournament. I'd mentioned it to Carla, but now I felt there was something even more.

I walked to the lodge and thought about the questions that needed to be answered. How did Cindy's death tie in? Who would use the Russian phrase *Do zavtra* and why? What were Jake and Wendy arguing about? Did *it* tie in? Where was Chief Blunt?

None of the questions were answered while I ate my breakfast.

Carla and Morphy were on the road. Perry was probably downstairs at that very moment arranging spectator chairs around the table and my opponent surely wasn't thinking about the deaths of Dan Tilley or Cal Pederson. He was thinking chess and that's what I needed to do.

The only difference in the playing hall compared to the rest of the tournament was that all of the folding tables had been collapsed and stacked against the far wall. In the middle of the room stood a rectangular table I guessed was from the dining room upstairs as it appeared to be suitable for four guests. A wood chessboard had been placed in the center of the table and was manned with a beautiful set of ebony and boxwood pieces carved in the traditional Staunton style. Two chairs were placed one on each side for the players (more dining room furniture I expected) and two rows of folding chairs were lined up to face a large display board on an easel where Perry would mimic the game with paper pieces.

I saw my opponent, Don Fitzgerald, Vick Tomlinson's adversary who'd stared me down at the beginning of the previous round, talking quietly with Perry and walked over to them. "Are you two conspiring against me?" I asked. There were handshakes all around and then it was quiet. "Did I interrupt something?"

Perry shook his head. "No, no. We were just discussing whether or not today's World Champion could beat Capablanca."

Jose Raul Capablanca was the World Chess Champion from 1921 to 1927 and considered one of the best chess players of all time. He had a penchant for positional play and was often the topic of such comparisons. I raised my eyebrows at them. "Interesting. Why aren't you putting him up against Fischer?"

Don frowned and shook his head. "There's no way he'd beat Fischer."

"Oh?" Perry said.

"Obviously. Fisher's analytical capabilities were far superior to anyone since. Besides, people always compare whoever happens to be the current World Champion to Fischer. Why is that?"

I shrugged and feigned innocence. "Maybe because instead of being thought of as one of the best he was considered to be *the* best. And since he never defended his title it's hard to prove him anything but the best."

Perry nodded. "So how about it Ray? Current World Champ vs. Capablanca. Who wins?"

"Honestly, I think between those two, one of them would win." I smiled and patted him on the back. "I have a game of my own to think about."

I wandered over to the board on the table, admired the pieces and listened to Don and Perry carry on. Past vs. present arguments seemed pointless to me in most categories because the circumstances for each person was different, often vastly. In chess it's meaningless to compare the likes of Fischer and anyone who came before him. Not because Fischer was superior (which an argument can usually be made for), but because he had the advantage of being able to study the styles, strategies, and tactical brilliancies of all the great players before him.

In effect, Fischer would know Capablanca's chess better than Capablanca would.

I also know the next line is, *Fischer would have to play without any knowledge of Capablanca*. But that is unfair because without having studied Capablanca there is no Fischer. It's the culmination of studying those who came before him paired with his own chess gifts that make Fischer the player he was.

I shook my head to clear the science fiction wormhole knots from my thoughts. Maybe that was Don's plan all along, to get my brain wrapped around something other than our game, just like the staring match. I walked back over to where he and Perry were talking. "You guys ever get a song stuck in your head?" They looked at me like I'd just ordered a hamburger in a Chinese restaurant. "The songs that really get stuck are the kind where the chorus just goes round and round. You know?" I sang some KC and the Sunshine Band, "*That's the way, uh huh uh huh, I like it, uh huh uh huh. That's the way, uh huh uh huh, I like it, uh huh uh huh.*" I looked at Don. "You know that one? Try it. You'll see what I mean."

I turned to hide my smile and went back to the table. It was time to play chess.

The time controls for the championship round were the same as the rest of the tournament had been: one hundred and twenty minutes per player for their first forty moves and another sixty minutes each for the remainder of the game. Usually one hundred and twenty minutes was more than enough time for local matches such as the Cedar Lake Chess Tournament, but I wasn't going to take Don for granted.

I heard voices in the stairwell and looked over my shoulder. Several people were coming down the stairs. Many were players from the tournament. There was

Smudge, Vick Tomlinson, and Leonard Nail accompanied by his daughter. Apparently she didn't have any hard feelings about being fired. I recognized some of the other hotel guests from having been around the lodge for the past week. A few of them looked confused as to what was going on. They'd probably just followed the crowd downstairs to see what the hubbub was. Some sat down on the folding chairs; others turned and headed back upstairs.

"Where's Carla?" Carey Nail asked as she came up behind me.

"She's on a day trip to Boise."

"She didn't want to watch you play?"

I shrugged. Truth was Carla had watched me play a lot of chess over the years and the Cedar Lake Tournament was supposed to be a vacation for both of us. "She didn't want to make me nervous. She gets all rowdy and shouts at the other player like she does when she watches football on TV. It's embarrassing."

Carey laughed. "Really?"

"No, not really." I smiled.

"My dad and I want to wish you luck."

"Thanks. I appreciate that."

She turned and sat down next to Leonard and I realized he was the person I needed to talk to. "Leonard," I said stepping over to him, "can I ask you a quick question?"

"Sure," he said, "but if it's about chess I don't think you need my help."

I gave him and his daughter a reassuring smile. "No, it's not about chess, Leonard. It's about when you were the assistant football coach."

Given the likely fact a murderer was in the room, I spoke quietly and while Leonard answered my question I chanced a glance at Perry. He nodded at me and motioned for Don and me to meet him at the table in the center of the room. "Thanks, Leonard. I really appreciate your help. I need to go play some chess now."

"Ladies and gentlemen," Perry said, "if I could have your attention we'll get the championship round of the 7th Annual Cedar Lake Chess Tournament underway." A few people applauded and he went on. "Before we get started however, I'd like to have a moment of silence to remember our friend and fellow chess player, Cal Pederson. As most of you know, Cal was taken from this world just a few days ago."

Perry bowed his head as did everyone in the audience. I looked at the floor a bit but then took the opportunity to scan the room for anyone who obviously felt no remorse or wanted to see how his (or *her*, Carla!) crime affected these people. Then I bowed my head fully as I remembered that Cal had most likely been mistakenly killed and his murderer was—hopefully—genuinely sorrowful.

"Thank you," Perry said. "Now, it's time for chess."

He introduced Don and me and then explained to the spectators the choosing of the color. Perry had Don and I face each other and then he took a white pawn and a black pawn from the board. He walked behind Don, who put his hands behind his back, and Perry placed a pawn in each of Don's open palms. Don mixed them around by passing them back and forth and then brought his closed fists around and aimed them at me. I pointed at his left hand. Don turned his left hand face up and opened his fist to reveal the white pawn. For the championship round I would play with the white pieces, which meant I would move first.

I smiled. "That's the way, uh-huh, uh-huh, I like it," I sang just loud enough for Don to hear.

37

■ We'd been playing for a few hours and it was time for lunch. A little after noon Perry announced we would adjourn for one hour. It was Don's turn so when he was ready Perry gave him a note card and asked him to write his move on it. Then Don sealed the card in an envelope and handed it back to Perry. By sealing the move it allowed us to adjourn the game without either player able to take advantage of the time away from the board. The move Don wrote down was his official move; he could not change his mind once we resumed the game. Similarly, while I had an idea of what my opponent's move might be, I didn't know for sure so I could not spend my lunch hour preparing for anything specific.

Perry stopped the clocks and everyone stood, stretched and made their way up the stairs. It was like we had all been in a cave for hours and were staggering up towards the light.

My first inclination was to call Carla and find out if she'd discovered anything in Boise, or if they'd even arrived yet. I checked my watch and decided she still had a half hour or so to drive. Besides, I didn't have any cell coverage and I didn't want to use the lobby phone.

I went outside for some fresh air and walked a couple laps around the lodge. The cool autumn air was a welcome relief from the stuffy basement where the game was being played and it gave my brain a jump start. I mentally went over the match as we'd played it so far and thought my plan was sound. I had a two pawn advantage and was confident I'd come out on top.

When my stomach rumbled like an angry bear I realized air wasn't the only thing I needed. The maple trees around the lake displayed their own renditions of red, orange and yellow against the deep green canvas of mountain firs. Clouds crowded the highest peaks and blustery gusts came off the lake and reached inside my jacket like a TSA pat down. I shivered, went back inside the lodge and ordered a cheeseburger and a salad. No fries. I didn't need my faculties all wishy washy in grease and carbohydrates. Time and place for everything and all that.

One thing I believed in whenever I played a long game of chess was if and when there was an adjournment, no matter for what amount of time, I needed to use it to clear my head, to *not* think about the upcoming moves the entire time. A quick once over was fine, but I didn't want to dwell on it and end up in a mental quagmire. Usually I would read a book or do something more physical like a short bike ride, a walk, or shoot a game of pool if a table was nearby. During the adjournment of the Cedar Lake Chess Championship round I had a murder case to wrap my brain around.

There was a chance I was wrong about the killer being a chess fan in 1972. If that were the case we'd be in big trouble because even in a small town like Jasper, Oregon, finding a murderer linked to 1972 without any sort of evidence would be very tough. Chess was the connection. I believed it like I believed Pluto was still a planet. The tournament I was currently playing in and the Russian note via Bobby Fischer's muttered phrase to Boris Spassky in 1972 wasn't a coincidence. The Cedar Lake Chess Tournament had somehow helped resurrect a murderer. It made no sense otherwise.

I took out my pen and organized my thoughts on a napkin. I felt like I was in a detective show, listing my suspects as if I were in charge and in complete control of whatever events still had yet to unfold.

"Gordon."

I looked up and saw Vick Tomlinson. "Vick. How are you doing?"

He nodded and I took that to mean he was doing okay. "I'm not going to say anything about the game. I know you know what you're doing. Just wanted to say good luck."

"Thanks." We shook hands and I saw him look down at my doodled-over napkin. His gaze rose back up and we looked at one another for a moment. He nodded again and walked away.

What was that *about?* I looked at my scribblings and saw at the bottom, *VT license plate*. Had he noticed? Was there actually something to the out of state car theory?

Fewer people returned after lunch to witness the remainder of the chess game. I told myself it was probably due to the restaurants in town serving their food too slowly. Not a big deal. I was there to play chess, they weren't. Most of the spectators who did return were the other *chess-cationers* who'd been knocked out of the tournament earlier, but only a few of the other hotel guests. Leonard was there, but his daughter wasn't. Smudge had a fresh bag of chips and I noticed Vick hadn't come back down.

Perry asked everyone to take their seats and quiet down. He directed Don and I to sit at the board, stood between us and ceremoniously withdrew the sealed envelope with Don's move inside from his jacket pocket. He tore open the end of the envelope and blew inside to puff it up. It was classic Johnny Carson as *Karnack* but I wasn't sure if that was Perry's intention. He removed the card and read out loud, "For his 24th move, Mr. Fitzgerald plays Rook to f5." Perry moved the Rook to the designated square and pressed the plunger to start my clock. Then he made the same move on the display board so the audience could see what Don had played.

BLACK

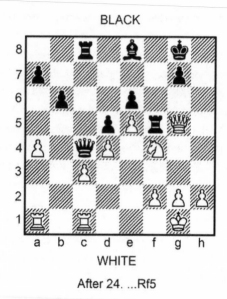

WHITE

After 24. ...Rf5

Rook to f5 was not a surprise. It's the move I expected since it threatened my Queen and Knight. I had mentally prepared a reply for it before the adjournment, but double-checked the position to make sure I hadn't missed anything. I nodded to myself and pulled my Queen to g3.

As much as I was focused on the chess game, whenever I had a moment I would look over at the people who were there to watch us and I wondered which one of them had killed Cal Pederson. Who among them had a hatred so deep he still intended to murder Jake Humboldt? Or did he? Had he given up after killing Cal by mistake? Seen the error of his ways, as it were?

Somehow I didn't think so. Whoever it was had been biding his time since 1972, a long time to develop a permanent psychological mechanism to kill. No, the killer was still here looking for an opportunity or developing a plan to strike again.

The *thunk!* of the clock plunger pulled my attention back to the game. Don had moved his Bishop to the f7 square at the corner of the board. It was a fine move but again, not unexpected. Bishops covered a lot of squares from the long diagonals of the board so it was sometimes advantageous to post them there, but not always. Don's problem was he didn't have his position fortified enough to keep me from bringing in my pieces and wreaking havoc.

Fortified position.

The killer was fortifying his position while everyone else was at the chess match. It wasn't who was here, it was who *wasn't*.

38

■ About a half hour after the chess match ended I found myself in the lobby of the Cedar Lake Lodge. A fire crackled in the massive river stone hearth and I sat in front of it staring up at Otto the moose.

"Ray? You okay?"

I turned away from the stuffed head with the claw marks still clear on the snout and looked at Perry Whitton. "Sure. Just tired. Have a seat."

"Hey, I'm sorry about what happened at the end there," he said as he eased himself into a boxy chair across from me. "I hope it didn't ruin the entire tournament for you."

"Perry, please tell me you didn't forget that Cal Pederson was murdered. Don't you think that was really the low point?"

"Of course I haven't forgotten about Cal. I'm just thinking of you right now. With everything else that's happened chess seems rather anti-climactic at this point."

I shrugged. He was right. "Have you seen Jake?"

"He's in the office. Why?"

"Do he and Wendy live here? In the lodge I mean."

He nodded. "Back behind the office. They did a lot of remodeling and now they basically live in the entire north side. There are no rooms for rent over there. If you go outside and look in any of the windows on that end of the lodge you'll be looking into their home."

I wondered if the killer had sat out in the woods and looked through those windows and into the lives of Jake and Wendy Humboldt. It seemed a rifle with a scope and an open curtain would be much simpler, quicker, easier to get away, and frankly, less messy. The werewolf story was convenient, but there was something else going on, something personal. The killer wanted more than these guys dead, he wanted to watch it happen. Up close.

"Ray?"

"Yeah?"

"You drifted off there for a second."

"Sorry. Just thinking."

"Anything I can help with?"

I shook my head but I wasn't really saying no. I just wasn't sure what my next move was. What was I missing that would clue me in to who wanted a group of former high school jocks dead now? And why? Was there anything Perry Whitton could offer that would help? "I don't know, Perry. I'm missing a piece or two from this puzzle. Or maybe I have the pieces but I don't know what the picture is. You know?"

"Have you talked to Bill?"

I shook my head. "I haven't seen him for days. Besides, cops don't like amateurs nosing around their cases. He made that pretty clear."

"What do you mean? I thought you two were seeing eye to eye after the meeting at my house."

"He agreed with the idea that Cal was mistaken for Jake, but I don't think he was ready to go into business together. Let me ask you though, have you seen Chief Blunt recently? Unlike me and him, you two *are* friends."

Perry looked at the fire while he thought. "I haven't, but I've been here with the chess tournament and all."

"I've been to the police station twice in the last few days and both times he was out. Yet before he always happened to be in. Does that sound normal? That he would suddenly be out and unavailable this long?"

"No. No, it doesn't."

"Can you call his wife and see if she knows anything?"

He shook his head. "Divorced. She left years ago for the excitement of the big city."

"How about the other cops? Will they tell you if you ask?"

"Probably. I know most of them well enough."

He pushed himself out of the chair and went over to the front desk where the landline phone was plugged in. I watched him chat with Wendy for a moment and then he picked up the phone.

I turned my attention back to the fire. Carla and Debbie were surely on their way back from Boise. More and more I hoped Carla had found some tidbit of information that might help with the case. With two people in Jasper dead, one in Portland and one we believed to be next on the list, some sort of clue would be nice.

Perry came back and sat down. He looked like he was visiting a friend in the hospital. "What did they say?" I asked.

He looked at me and leaned forward, glanced around the room to see who might be listening. "They don't know where he is," he whispered. "They haven't heard from him since Thursday."

"What? How does that happen?"

Perry shrugged but his knee bounced up and down like a jackhammer and he rubbed his hands over each other as he stared back at me. He shook his head and gazed into the fire.

"Perry." He looked back at me. "Are the police looking for him?"

He nodded. "Under the radar. I think they're pretty worried about it. Bill doesn't just leave."

"It's got to be related to these murders."

"Of course it does. That's all he's been working on or talking about."

"Who's in charge now?" I asked.

"A guy by the name of Lt. Pitt."

I nodded. "I've met him, seems straight up. Will he let us help?"

"Might."

"We need to get into Chief Blunt's office and his home."

Perry frowned in confusion. "Why?"

"To see if he left any notes or anything that might tell us where he went or what he was doing before he vanished."

"I'm sure Pitt has already done that."

I nodded. "He probably checked the office, but maybe not his house. Being divorced the Chief probably does a lot of his thinking at home. Worth a shot anyway, right?"

He nodded and stood up. "I'll drive."

39

◾ Officer Angela Drake, the suspicious desk duty cop who'd given Carla and me the silent treatment at the police station, was put in charge of letting Perry and me into the Chief's house.

Bill Blunt lived in a smallish two-bedroom home with an attached garage and a backyard that would have had Morphy begging me to throw a tennis ball. The house itself was drill-sergeant green with white trim. The covered front porch ran the width of the house and there was a deck out back. It was one level but the foundation rose high enough for seven concrete steps to march up to the front door. A U.S. flag hung limply from one of the porch columns and several jack-o-lanterns grinned from the ends of the steps.

We'd finished our perimeter check of the house and determined there was no sign of forced entry and the Chief's car was not in the garage. Officer Drake pulled a set of keys from her jacket pocket and unlocked the door. She withdrew her 9mm from its holster, pushed the door open with her toe and stepped inside. "Bill," she called, "I know you're not here, but if you or someone else is, this is Officer Drake and I'm coming inside."

"How do you know he's not here?" Perry asked.

"We've been calling here and his cell hourly. I was here yesterday too, just to make sure he wasn't dead."

I nodded to myself. It was nice to know she'd checked. "Did you find anything else?" I asked. "Something that might give us an idea of where he is?"

She holstered her weapon and shook her head. "Nope. Didn't look for anything. Honestly I just wanted to make sure he hadn't had a heart attack or a stroke or something."

"Okay. If he's got a home office that would be the first place to look."

"Over here," Perry said and led us into what had once been the dining room. Instead of a large table and chairs though, there was a desk littered with papers, envelopes, an empty coffee mug, and a stack of manila file folders.

"I guess his system is different here than at work," Drake said.

I smiled. "Not the neat freak you know?"

She shook her head.

"Come on," Perry said and stepped behind the desk. "What are we looking for?"

"Probably a note or a notebook, probably somewhere on the desk, not in a drawer. Unless you find a folder with Dan Tilley's or Cal Pederson's name. Might be something in there too. Just look for anything related to the case, current dates or names you recognize."

Perry shuffled through the loose papers on top of the desk, but Officer Drake didn't move. I looked at her and caught her staring back. She had a *who* are *you?* kind of look on her face. "People like Chief Blunt write things down," I said and waved my hand at the desk. "He keeps track of what he's done, and if it's something that involves a case, what he plans to do as well. A checklist if you will." She nodded but stayed put, much like she had been behind the desk at the police station. "And I watch Sherlock Holmes on PBS."

Drake frowned and shook her head and turned into the kitchen. No sense of humor. I stood on the other side of the desk and rummaged with Perry.

"There's nothing here," Perry said. "Mostly home office stuff: bills, taxes, receipts. No notes."

"No police business at all?"

"This." Perry had a baby blue Post-It Note stuck to his index finger and he reached it across the desk to me. I pulled it away and read, *Check out Ray Gordon, Seattle P.D.*

"Seriously? That's all?"

"Nothing else I can find."

"Is there anywhere else in this house he spends time? Kitchen maybe? In front of the TV?"

"Find anything, Angela?" Perry called.

Drake stepped back into the home office. "No. Nothing in there."

"I'm going to take Ray down to the basement."

"What's down there?" she asked.

"You don't know?"

She shook her head. "Should I?"

"How long have you been a Jasper cop?"

"Three years. Four in April."

He nodded. "Long enough. I'm sure Bill won't mind you knowing."

Drake looked at me and we shared a moment of mutual piqued interest. Perry made it sound like Bill Blunt had a secret. What could be in the basement? A home movie theater? Game room? Workshop? A torture chamber?

"Follow me," Perry said and walked into the kitchen where he opened a door, clicked on a light and headed down the stairs. I went next, slowly. Basements weren't exactly my favorite places and since Perry didn't allude to what was in store for us, I went warily, a fox checking each step toward the hen house.

Drake came behind me and she wasn't in a rush either. For every two steps I took, she came down one. I was just waiting to hear the rasp of metal against leather as she withdrew her gun from its holster.

Perry made it to the bottom of the stairs and I heard a series of clicks. Cold fluorescent light glowed from the basement ceiling that was still below Drake's and my feet. With the lights beyond the stairwell on, I picked up my pace and when I finally saw below the ceiling and what awaited us I practically ran down the steps.

Perry smiled as I joined him and we both turned to catch Officer Drake's reaction. She came down the stairs into the basement and didn't even see us, her attention drawn to the scene around her. "Oh, wow," she said.

About waist high a miniature world filled the entire basement. Right in front of us was a town with streets, traffic signals, businesses, cars and tiny people. In the corners mountains rose to the ceiling and through it all ran small-scale trains.

Jasper's Chief of Police was a model railroader.

Perry led us around the staircase toward the back of the room. We passed a farm whose barn was in need of new red paint and a few horses milled around a man fixing an old tractor. There was a logging facility up in the mountains and in the very back was a long lake with a replica of the Humboldt's lodge at the far end.

"Is this a past version of Jasper?" I asked.

Perry shook his head. "No. There are a few buildings and areas that Bill modeled after the real deal, but the landscape, town, all of it, he just built on his own."

"This is incredible," Drake said. "Look at the detail." She pointed at the lake where a fisherman in a boat had a trout arched inside a net. There was even a splash where the fish had been lifted out of the water.

"Can we see the trains go?" I asked Perry.

He smiled. "I'd love to, but no. Bill is a serious railroader. He actually has schedules for the trains and if they're in the wrong place he'll kill me."

Drake straightened up and the smile on her face fell away. "Why did you bring us down here?"

"Right," Perry said. "Over here." Tucked beneath the stairs was an old desk with a wooden swivel chair. Perry clicked on the desk lamp. "If he's not upstairs he's here. In fact, I believe he spends more time down here."

I sat in the chair and looked over the desk. On my left was an old wire-bound notebook labeled *Timetables*. I thumbed through it but it looked like jibberish to my untrained eyes. Perry took it and confirmed the lines of numbers were the schedules he'd just told us about. Next to the desk lamp was a tray of small tools, a tube of modeling cement and a few strips of fine sandpaper. On the right side of the desk was a large magnifying glass on a mount so it could be adjusted and used hands free. "Does Chief Blunt build his sets and trains here?" I asked Perry.

"Most of them. Not the big stuff like the mountains of course. The landscape gets built where it ends up, but yeah, the buildings, people and individual things."

"This is his hobby, his escape," I said and looked at Drake. "He wouldn't bring his work here, to this space."

She shook her head. "I wouldn't."

The radio attached to her shoulder squawked and a tinny voice said, "Code thirty, code thirty. Officer needs emergency assistance."

Drake thumbed the switch and said, "This is Drake. What have you got, Cooper?"

There was silence and then, "It's the Chief, Drake. Someone found him alongside the road out on route 16 by the hikers parking area. He's in bad shape."

"I'm on my way," she said and ran up the stairs.

40

■ Perry drove his 1960s era Chevrolet pickup and did his best to keep up with Officer Drake's police cruiser. She was well ahead of us, sirens screaming, lights whirling and would soon lose us over the next hill, but Perry knew where she was going. We were on a straight stretch of two-lane highway headed due west from Jasper's small airfield and the scattered pine trees had thickened into a forest.

"How much farther?" I asked.

"Ten minutes," Perry said. His hands white knuckled around the steering wheel.

"Is that real time or because we're going uphill?" He glared at me and then turned his gaze back to the road. "Sorry," I said. "Just trying to lighten the mood." *Don't joke about the man's truck*, I thought. *Check*.

The flashing red and blue lights of Drake's police car were gone. She'd disappeared over the hill and when we reached the same point she was nowhere in sight. "Three more turns through these S curves and we'll be there," Perry said. "It's an old railroad bed people use as a hiking trail now."

He's in pretty bad shape is what I'd heard the police dispatcher say over Drake's radio. What did that mean other than Chief Blunt was hurt? What had happened? Had he been attacked or was he in an accident?

"Perry, does Chief Blunt come up here to hike?"

"Sometimes, but only on the weekends."

"He *never* comes up here during the week?

"Not that I know of, but I'm not his damn wife."

I nodded. *Understood.* He was worried and he had every right to be. His friend had been found *in bad shape.* For all Perry knew, Chief Blunt was on the verge of death and he hadn't even known the man had been missing.

Perry slowed just enough to not roll the truck and pulled the old Chevy off the highway and up into a corridor of tall fir trees. The afternoon light dimmed as it filtered through the thick forest and made it easy to spot Drake's police cruiser about three hundred yards ahead. She'd pulled off the road into a clearing but left her lights on.

Perry brought the truck to a brake-squealing stop and we both jumped out. An ambulance was backed in and blocked the trailhead. It was eerily quiet and I looked at Perry and shrugged, then Drake stepped out from behind the ambulance and waved us over.

"They haven't loaded him up yet," she said. "He's being macho and wants to ride back into town with me."

Perry shook his head. "Stubborn old goat. He'll walk back if you don't give him a ride."

"No way. He's going to the hospital whether he likes it or not. He's got a deep gash and a lump on the back of his head the size of a softball. The EMTs are surprised he's not in a coma."

"What happened?" I asked.

"Got hit from behind. When he came to he was tied up in a cabin."

"Who did it?"

She shrugged.

"What's that supposed to mean?" Perry asked and mimicked her shrug. "There's more to this story. People in Jasper don't just go around clubbing policemen and hiding them in the woods."

"It's all I've gotten out of him so far."

Perry huffed and went around to the back of the ambulance. I looked at Drake and she tilted her head to follow.

Chief Blunt lay on a gurney, but it had been lifted at one end so he was sitting up. His face was caked with mud and dried blood and a brilliant white bandage was held to the back of his head by a few turns of gauze. There were about four blankets around him and he held them up to his chin and shivered every few seconds. He looked like the photograph of a victim who'd been pulled out of a war zone.

"We're finished here," one of the EMTs said to Drake.

She nodded. "Okay, let's get him out of here."

Blunt made an effort to swing his legs over the side of the gurney but Perry held him down by the shoulder. "Let go of me," the Chief said.

Drake stepped in front of her boss with one hand on her holstered weapon. She jabbed her other finger at him and said, "I swear to God I will shoot you."

Blunt looked shocked. "I will remind you that I am still the Chief of Police here."

"And if I was the one on that gurney, or anyone else for that matter, you would make them go to the hospital, right? And you'd make them go in the ambulance. In fact, you probably would have already shot them. Am I right?" Blunt scowled but didn't say anything. "That's what I thought."

My opinion of Officer Angela Drake made a sudden 180° turn from what I'd thought of her before. Her no-nonsense attitude reminded me of Carla.

The EMTs loaded the gurney and Chief Blunt as one into the ambulance. "Want some company?" I asked.

He shook his head. "We need to talk though. Perry, will you bring him by in an hour or so? Drake, you meet me at the hospital. We'll talk first."

It was around 5pm when Perry and I walked into Chief Blunt's hospital room. He was cleaned up, had a new bandage wound around his head and wore a hospital gown.

"How are you feeling, Bill?" Perry asked.

"Annoyed mostly. A bit pissed off. Not as dizzy, which is good."

"Dizzy?" I asked.

Blunt pointed to his head. "Concussion. Got whacked pretty good."

"Okay," Perry said and pulled up a chair. "Let's start from the beginning. What happened?"

Blunt looked at me. I wasn't sure if he wanted me to sit down or to leave. I sat down next to Perry and crossed my arms.

"I went to check that name you left me," Blunt said to me, "the one with the Idaho license plate. I knew the guy was staying out at the Blue Bucket. I went out there but never even got to his room. Somebody stuck what he said was a gun in my back and asked what I was doing there."

"Was it Vick Tomlinson?" I asked.

"I don't know," he sighed. "I never got a look at him and I didn't recognize the voice. Anyway, I had my hands up and told him I was only there to talk to someone, not to detain. Then he reached for my gun." Blunt shook his head. "That's when it gets real, you know? I couldn't let him just take my firearm so we fought over it. Struggled really. He wrestled it out of my hand and then hit me, with my own gun I assume. Ain't that somethin'? Hurt like hell too. I did manage to release the clip though, before he got the upper hand on me. I threw it out into the parking lot, but then he conked me so I don't know if he retrieved it or not. If he did, he's got fifteen rounds. If not, he's got the one that was up the pipe. If we're lucky he doesn't know much about handguns and didn't realize what I did."

"And you woke up in the cabin?" Perry prompted.

Blunt nodded. "Tied up but there was a water bottle and a couple of granola bars within reach."

"Could you tell whose cabin it was?" I asked.

"It was the old Smyth cabin." He looked at Perry and they shared a knowing nod. "Teenagers go up there to fool around. Everyone knows about it. Next strong wind will blow it over."

Perry shook his head. "Why didn't you tell anyone where you were going? You could be dead right now and no one would know it. None of your cops knew anything."

Blunt studied his fingers. "It was the end of the day and to be honest, I didn't think there was much to it." He looked at me. "An out of state license plate, right? What's the big deal?"

I shrugged. "How did you get out of the cabin?"

"The knots weren't tight, but he did hit me pretty hard. I couldn't see straight or stand up without falling over for a long time. When I ran out of water and granola bars I had to do something. I was still dizzy so I crawled. All the way down the mountain. Blind luck I came across those hikers."

"Unfortunately we still don't know a damn thing," Perry said and stood up.

I shook my head. "Not true, Perry. We know he's not willing to kill just anyone. He wouldn't have left food and water for Chief Blunt otherwise. He just needed him out of the way, which means he'll go after Jake very soon."

"I've got an officer out at the lodge in plain clothes right now," Blunt said.

I nodded. "Good. We also know he wants to be up close and personal with his victims. The whole werewolf thing plays here but I'm still not sure why. That all may change now that he has a gun. If he's desperate he may use it instead of a knife. It would help to know if he has your clip or not."

"We do know." We turned toward the door and Officer Drake walked in. She held up her hand and dangled a long rectangular clip full of 9mm rounds. "He's got one shot," she said.

41

The lobby of the Cedar Lake Lodge was surprisingly busy for the time of day. Because of the chess tournament there were a few people with suitcases and bags checking out late and others, locals I guessed, were there for dinner or drinks.

Perry and I had checked on Jake and Wendy as soon as we'd arrived. As far as they were concerned, it was business as usual, though they were worried about Chief Blunt. We sat in the lobby and looked at each other. "Now what?" Perry asked.

"Now we wait to see what happens."

"We wait for Jake to get murdered? Let's just grab Vick."

I shook my head. "You know the police can't arrest him. Chief Blunt couldn't ID his attacker, and just because he was on his way to talk to Vick doesn't mean Vick was the one who hit him." Perry harrumphed and crossed his arms. "Do you know the cop Chief Blunt sent over here?" I asked.

He nodded toward the corner where a young man in his mid to late 20s was fiddling with his phone. He was wearing jeans, a black and red flannel shirt, and hiking boots. "Not bad," I said. "Looks like he's here for the trails."

"He probably jumped at the chance to go under cover. I'm sure he's only seen it done in the movies." He looked around and said, "Where's Carla? I haven't seen her all day."

"She went to Boise. When we didn't hear anything from Chief Blunt about the license plate, we kind of took it upon ourselves to get some information. The name the car was registered under isn't Vick Tomlinson. It's Peter Mitchell. Does that name mean anything to you?" Perry looked at the floor and then back at me, shook his head. "We called the courthouse in Boise and they said there was a sealed record involved and we could look at it, but only in person. Carla wanted to check it out. I didn't think there was much to it, but now after what happened to the Chief…" I shrugged.

"Have you heard from her?"

I shook my head. "No service out here and you know what happened to my phone at the end of the match. She should be back any minute though."

Vick Tomlinson came into the lodge and nodded at me and Perry. We nodded back and watched as he went over and sat next to Kevin Corsmo. They sat with their backs to us and Perry just stared. "Son of a bitch," he mumbled. "I should go club him over the head with that lamp he's sitting next to."

"Tempting," I said.

"You know, I have no idea why we're all here, you, me and the cop over there. Vick isn't going to do anything here in the lobby with all of these people around."

"They'll be gone sooner or later. I know what you mean though. Sitting here with the guy we think is a murderer makes me a little jumpy too."

"How about a drink? I'm buying."

I nodded. "Sure. Whatever you're having."

Perry walked over to the bar and I watched as he ordered. The drinks were made quickly and I wondered if it was because of who Perry was, or just a lack of business. Most of the guests were moving into the dining room.

Perry came back with a tumbler in each hand and gave me one. "Scotch and water," he said.

"Thanks."

We sipped our drinks in silence and I wondered about Carla. Where was she? I was sure she had probably tried to call. Even if she didn't have any news from the courthouse, she would have wanted to know how the tournament ended. I thought about Chief Blunt too and where he was attacked. "How familiar are you with the Blue Bucket Inn?" I asked Perry.

"Familiar enough I suppose. They're not featured in the Jasper travel brochure, but what do you want to know?"

"Do they have security cameras? Has anyone gone over to see if there were any witnesses to the Chief's attack?"

"No and yes. A place like that doesn't even have the fake cameras. Drake went over there as soon as she got back, remember? She went to look for the clip and to knock on doors. No one saw or heard a thing." I didn't remember hearing that and it must have showed on my face. "We were leaving Bill's room and you were already halfway down the hall when she told me," Perry said.

"Do you know who else is staying there? From the chess tournament I mean?"

He shook his head and took a drink. "I only got home addresses and phone numbers from the players. Jake and Wendy gave them a discounted rate if they stayed here, but not all of them were able to. Why?"

"Just trying to narrow the field if I can."

"I thought your theory was Vick Tomlinson?" he whispered.

I shrugged, remembering my thoughts during the chess game earlier in the day. It was who *wasn't* there, not who was. Vick Tomlinson had been in the front row, at least before the adjournment. "I want to be sure," I said.

One of the big double doors opened then and Carla stepped inside. She looked around the lobby but she didn't smile when she saw me. I looked at Perry. "Uh oh."

Carla rushed over, leaned over the back of the couch between Perry and me and gave me a kiss. "Hi," she said with a smile.

"Hi. How was the—"

"Did you win? I tried to call but you didn't answer. I did leave a message."

"My phone—"

"Tell me! Did you win?"

"Sorry to intrude," Perry said and sat forward enough so he could turn and see us both, "but Carla, what did you find out? We need to put this whole thing to rest as soon as possible."

She looked him and then at me. "Well, it wasn't Vick Tomlinson."

42

■ "What?" I asked Carla. "What do you mean, *it wasn't Vick Tomlinson?*"

She shrugged. "I suppose he *could* still be the killer, but I don't think so. The car is definitely not his either." She smiled.

"Okay, what did you find?" Perry asked.

"We already knew the license plate is registered under someone named Peter Mitchell, right?" I nodded.

"Do you remember the sealed file?" I nodded. "Peter Mitchell isn't his real name. It's Eric *Bickerman*. He's Cindy Bickerman's little brother. His real name is Eric Peter Bickerman, but after Cindy was killed the rest of the family moved to Boise and he used his middle name and then legally took his mother's maiden name to get away from all of the questions about Cindy."

Carla's revelation was the key I'd been searching for. Suddenly all of the doors in my brain opened up and the clues, information, pictures, memories, suspicions, just everything came rushing out to come together in one cohesive case. I held my head and closed my eyes. Everything about the Jasper murders, 1972 and present, made sense. The only thing left was to figure out who Cindy's little brother was. I looked at Perry. "Where's the list of chess players?"

"We checked all of them. No one from Boise is playing in the tournament and there were no Bickermans or Mitchells."

"Could he have played under an assumed name?" Carla asked.

I shook my head. "Not unless he's been doing it for years. The USCF keeps everyone's ratings updated. Wait, was everyone rated, Perry? Any new players?"

"Carla!"

We all turned toward the lobby doors where Debbie Mathews had just come in. She waved when she saw me then looked back at Carla. "Can I get my bag out of the car?"

"I'm parked right out front," Carla told me. "I'll be right back."

She went outside with Debbie and Perry looked at me. "She locked the car?" he asked.

I shrugged. "Habit. We're from a big city. So what about new players? Were there any?"

"No. Everyone checked out with the USCF."

I frowned. "I still think it's someone who…wait a minute. We checked everyone who entered the tournament, but not every chess player who was here."

Perry shook his head in confusion. "I think everyone in the tournament was a chess player, Ray. And if they were a chess player they were here to play in the tournament. What am I missing?"

"Kevin Corsmo," I said. "He's a chess player but he wasn't in the tournament. He could come and go as he pleased."

Perry and I stared at each other, our wheels spinning. Corsmo was the speed chess challenger who'd set up a table in the lobby since day one. Vick Tomlinson had sat down next to him just a few minutes earlier. Could they be working together?

"Where did he go?" Perry asked.

"Who?"

"Corsmo. He was right there a minute ago."

I glanced up. Vick Tomlinson was sitting alone.

"Ray! Ray!" It was a woman's frantic voice from outside, but it wasn't Carla's. Where *was* Carla? How long did it take to...wait. I was on my feet and out the door before I remembered there was an undercover cop in the lobby. Maybe he heard the woman scream my name. Maybe he would be curious why I ran outside, and follow me. Maybe it was nothing to worry about.

I was wrong.

The Land Cruiser was parked at the foot of the stairs; Debbie Mathews was standing a few feet away from the driver's side door. She pointed at the car when she saw me and said, "He's got Jake and Carla!"

43

■ Carla was behind the wheel of the Land Cruiser, Jake
was in the front passenger seat and Kevin Corsmo sat in
the middle of the backseat. It was dark but the light from
inside the lodge was enough for me to see the 9mm resting
against Carla's shoulder as Kevin said something to her.

There were voices behind me, around me. I didn't
know who they belonged to or if they were speaking to
me. Carla Caplicki, my best and truest friend, the woman
I'd finally admitted to myself and to her that I'd loved all
along, was in a car with a murderer. I couldn't hear what
Kevin said to her, but Carla shook her head. "Start it!" he
yelled, his voice muffled by the glass.

Carla's hands gripped the steering wheel and her
eyes were squeezed shut. "I can't!" she yelled back.

Kevin's fist shot forward and he hit Carla on the
back of the head with the gun. She screamed in surprise

and pain. My feet moved forward but someone grabbed my arms. "No, Ray!" someone said.

Then it happened. A blur of yellow fur came over the back seat with a growl and Morphy was on top of Carla's attacker. Corsmo screamed and disappeared from my site. Carla and Jake both turned in their seats and looked to be wrestling with either Corsmo or the dog.

"Get off!" Kevin yelled.

"Morphy!"

The car rocked back and forth and Morphy's yellow fur flashed in the light, his growls and barking audible to everyone. Inside the car it must have been unbearable. Carla climbed further over her seat and that's when I heard the shot.

Blood spattered against the windshield and Carla screamed. I threw an elbow and a punch at whoever was holding me, broke free and ran to the car.

The passenger door flung open and Jake tumbled out. I made for the driver's side and pulled open the door. Carla's back was to me as she was twisted around to face the back seat. Her body motionless.

I took a deep breath and touched her back. "Carla?" She moved, turned around and slid back down into the driver's seat. She opened her eyes and burst into tears. "Oh my god, Ray. I'm so sorry."

"Are you hurt?"

She shook her head. "Morphy."

I looked over her shoulder. Corsmo was gone. I had a brief recollection of someone, Drake I thought, pulling him out of the car while I checked on Carla. Morphy was there though, his front paws stretched toward the open rear passenger door while his back legs were twisted beneath him, one hanging over the seat. His head was between his front legs but listed to the right.

I ran around to the other side so I would be face to face with Morphy. His tongue lolled out of his open mouth and his eyes were unfocused. His chest and belly were matted with blood and his breaths were short and ragged. I put my hand in front of his nose and gently stroked his head. "Hey, Morph," I whispered.

Clarity swam back into his eyes and he looked at me. He coughed and tried to raise a paw but couldn't. I patted him, "It's okay, pal. It's okay." I looked over the seat. "Carla, get some help. Please! Hurry!"

Carla jumped out of the car but the logical part of my brain knew it was too late. No vet in town would make it out to the lodge in time to save Morphy. He was slipping away.

I held one hand over his wound in a desperate attempt to stop the bleeding. With the other I tugged on his ears and gently stroked the bridge of his nose. There was so much blood, it seeped through my fingers, and I gently pressed harder. Morphy took a shuddering breath and moved his paw towards me. I held it and I knew this was our goodbye. His body relaxed and his paw slipped out of my hand. "Thank you for being my friend, Morph," I whispered.

I leaned forward and hugged Morphy's body for what felt like a long time. I just didn't want him to leave. I remembered bringing him home from the shelter, sharing hamburgers from Red Mill and our long evenings watching movies with his head on my lap.

Carla touched my shoulder. She was crying. "Ray, I'm so sorry. Oh, Morphy."

Her words were a trigger. I pushed out of the back of the car and looked for Kevin Corsmo. People stood everywhere between me and the lodge doors. They were shapes really, I recognized no one. Then I saw him. Kevin

Corsmo was only a few yards away flanked by a cop and someone in plain clothes.

I took off at a full run and slammed into his body like a missile. We hit the ground with me on top and I unleashed every ounce of hell I could muster from within. Morphy was dead, Carla could have been killed and for the innocent lives he had taken, Corsmo needed to pay.

His nose crunched flat with my first blow and blood sprayed across his lips. I had both of his arms pinned under my knees and I pummeled his face, blindly swinging to let my fists land wherever they could. I felt my knuckle tear against his teeth and watched his eye begin to swell.

"Ray, that's enough!" It was a woman's voice but it wasn't Carla. "Ray!"

Before I could swing at Corsmo again both of my arms were grabbed from behind and I was lifted up. I was turned around and came face to face with Angela Drake. She was the unformed cop who'd stood next to Corsmo when I tackled him. I didn't remember her arriving on the scene.

"Ray?" she said. I was crying, heaving breaths and shaky. "Ray!" She held my chin and made me look at her. We stood like that for a few seconds and then she spun me around and walked me over to the Land Cruiser. Carla sat on the grass, leaned against the open door with Morphy on the seat above her. Drake pushed me toward Carla and said, "Stay over there."

I pulled Morphy's body from the back seat and hugged him to me as my own legs gave way and I slid to the ground next to Carla. She laid her head on my shoulder and put one hand on Morphy. We sat there together for I don't know how long and cried.

44

■ The Jasper City Police station was much more active with an alleged killer in custody. All of the police officers were there, even the off-duty cops. There was a reporter from the local paper and a few locals who wanted to get a look at who had been terrorizing them. They'd all heard about what had happened at Cedar Lake Lodge and wanted to be there when Kevin Corsmo, AKA Peter Mitchell, arrived from the hospital.

Perry Whitton brought Carla and me into town and we met Jake and Wendy Humboldt at the front entry of City Hall. Officer Drake led us through the throng of curious citizens toward the police department. We were subjected to stares and more than a few mumbled questions about who we were, if we were involved and why we got to go beyond the front desk.

I spotted Gabe Anderson and his pal who we thought had his throat slashed. They stood by the wall and when we saw each other, Gabe pushed his way over to me. "Hey, Ray. What's going on? We heard you got him."

I nodded. "Looks that way."

"They say he's at the hospital. What happened to him?"

I shrugged and smiled and Carla pulled me away into the crowd.

We went into a conference room and sat around the table like refugees. Jake and Wendy sat on the opposite side of the room from the door and huddled together. Perry sat at the end closest to the door while Carla and I sat on the corner next to him. Drake stood by the door. "Can I get anyone some coffee?" she asked.

Carla dropped her backpack on the floor and slumped in her chair. "Coffee would be great."

"I'm sure Bill has something stronger in his desk," Perry said.

"Yes," Wendy chimed in, "coffee please."

Drake poked her head out the door and asked one of the off-duty cops to brew a pot.

"So this whole time you were lying to me," Jake said.

I looked up and met his gaze. "About what?"

"About *what*? What do you think? Your dog, right? You let me buy you dinner."

"I paid for that afterward. Besides, I heard you're selling so what difference does it make?"

"We're talking about your dog, nothing else."

"I'm not really in the mood for this conversation, Jake."

"I don't care if you're in the mood. I—"

"Enough!" Drake slapped her palm on the table like a gavel. "From what I saw, Jake, you'd most likely be dead right now if it wasn't for that dog. Give it a rest. No dogs allowed in a mountain cabin is a stupid rule anyway."

He looked at her indignantly and put his arm around his wife who began to cry at the mention of his possible death. "What are we doing here anyway?" he asked. "We have things to do."

Like pack, I thought.

"Chief Blunt wants to chat," Drake said.

"*Chat*? What does that mean?"

Before any of us could offer up our definitions of the word *chat*, there was a murmur from the crowd gathered at the desk.

We looked at one another and Drake looked out the door. The rookie Anderson pushed his way into the conference room with a tray laden with cups and coffee makings. If he'd been wearing a tux he would have looked like a butler. He looked at Drake and said, "Chief's here." He placed the tray in the middle of the table and then stood in the corner…like a butler.

Drake looked out the door and then stepped aside as Chief Blunt led Kevin Corsmo toward the head of the table. Corsmo's hands were cuffed in front of him and his ankles were chained, making him shuffle in front of the Chief. His eyes were swollen and purple, there was a metal brace taped over his nose and another bandage covered a wound on his left cheekbone. I thought of Morphy and smiled as Chief Blunt pushed his prisoner into a chair.

"What's *he* doing here?" Jake demanded and pointed at Corsmo. "Put him in a cell for God's sake!"

"Jake Humboldt, I am the Chief of Police in this town. I do not presume to tell you how to run your hotel; you'll do the same for me."

"But—"

"I'm glad we understand each other."

Wendy put her hand on her husband's arm and Perry shook his head. Blunt looked at the handcuffed suspect. "Mr. Corsmo, I hear you used to live here many years ago and are in fact, the younger brother of Cindy Bickerman. True?"

Corsmo stared at the table and remained silent. Below the table, his knees were bouncing like pistons, their movement coursing up to his shoulders. Then he looked at Jake, hatred in his eyes. "Would it make a difference?" he asked.

"It might," said Blunt. "At least we could start to make some sense of all this."

"I think I can help you with that, Chief," I said.

"Ok, Gordon," Blunt said, "let's hear what you have."

Everyone at the table looked at me and Carla handed over her backpack. I slid out the 1972 Jasper High School yearbook along with Carla's copy of *Werewolves of the Western United States* and placed them on the table facing Corsmo. "I'm going to go through this quickly because frankly, I'd rather not be in the same room with you right now."

"Why?" Corsmo asked. "Because I defended myself against your dog? Wah, okay? My sister was butchered in the woods when she was fifteen. My dad blew his brains out a couple of years later and my mom slowly drank herself to death. So don't whine to me about your damn dog!"

Chief Blunt stood up just as Carla was about to fire back. "Okay, everyone," he said, "take a deep breath. Let's stick to why we're here. Gordon?" He sat back down, took a deep breath and nodded at me.

"Right," I said and opened *Werewolves of the Western United States* to the chapter dedicated to Cindy Bickerman. "Your sister was *butchered*, as you put it, on Saturday, October 21st, 1972. The officials at the time placed her death sometime between late afternoon and 9pm. Correct so far?" No one objected so I continued. "I've been told you and your sister were bullied as kids. In fact, two of your sister's tormentors are in this room right now."

All heads turned to the Humboldts. "It was a different world back then, right?" Jake said. "We didn't mean anything by it."

"That's what all bullies say when things get out of hand," Drake said.

"You had a pretty good idea of who killed your sister though, didn't you Kevin?" I asked. "Or should I call you Peter?" He looked at Jake but remained silent. "Okay, then. But when the police failed to make an arrest you decided it was up to you. You'd watched the coverage of the World Chess Championship and the phrase *do zavtra* seemed appropriate because being so young you couldn't do anything about it. Yet.

"My guess is that over the years you thought about revenge, about justice, probably plotted it all out but never acted on it. Then, about a month or more ago, you received a phone call. How am I doing so far?" No reaction. "Of course I have no idea what was said in that conversation, but it had something to do with money. The caller offered information that would lead to some kind of closure about your sister's death in exchange for money." Kevin said nothing but I caught a quick glance between Jake and Wendy. "The problem was you weren't sure who'd called you. Of course the caller couldn't give you his name, but something about what was said gave you the confidence that you'd been right all those years ago in assuming Jake Humboldt or one of his buddies, or all of them together, had murdered your sister. And here we are. You got all of them but one and here he sits. How frustrated you must be right now."

"Gordon," Blunt said.

"Sorry, Chief. Kevin, you were right about the call, it *was* Jake. Cedar Lake Lodge is in financial trouble and they were looking for some easy money. At least Jake was." The Humboldts stared at me and I stared right back.

"Everyone heard you two arguing that night," Carla said.

"Here's the bad news, Kevin." I opened up the yearbook to the football schedule and slid it across to him. "All of the men you thought had killed your sister were out of town playing football on October 21st. They were playing the Mountainview Cougars and didn't get home until after midnight according to Mr. Nail who was an assistant coach. None of them were involved in your sister's death."

Corsmo's face drained and I thought he might pass out. The evidence in front of him proved he'd murdered at least three innocent men, maybe four.

"You were close, Kevin," I said. "Not that it helps."

He looked up. "But he told me things. On the phone, he told me things only someone who'd been there would know. Things I knew that weren't in the reports, the necklace she wore that day."

"Think about it," I said. "If none of the football players killed Cindy, how would Jake know the details?"

He thought about it while he stared straight ahead. "Oh my God," he whispered. Then he bolted up and Chief Blunt grabbed his arm. Corsmo glared across the table. "She actually liked you! Of all your cliquey friends, she liked you! Not that any of you took the time to…"

Everyone looked at Wendy and she burst into tears. "I can't do this anymore," she wailed. "It was an accident! I'm so, so sorry."

"Looks like you have two killers in your midst, Chief," I said.

45

■ "How did you figure it out?" Perry asked me. His wife Della had returned the night before and they'd invited Carla and me over for lunch before we left for Seattle.

"Carla did it. As soon as she told me the car belonged to Cindy's little brother it all made sense. I had a suspicion her death and Dan Tilley's were connected by more than the werewolf story. Revenge is a powerful motive. I just needed that last piece."

"I almost feel sorry for him now," Carla said. "He lost his whole family."

"What about you, Carla?" Della asked. "Are you okay?"

Carla nodded. "I didn't believe he was going to hurt me. I never felt threatened by him anyway, even when he hit me. But I knew if I did what he wanted, if I drove away, Jake would end up dead." She took a deep breath and stared at the table, somehow seeing what had happened in the woodgrain. "I've never seen anyone so consumed. He was only about revenge, about killing the person he believed got away with killing his sister."

"He's been so focused his entire life," I mused, "I wonder if his mind even let him understand that he murdered the wrong people."

Della shook her head. "I've known Wendy since she was in high school. I just can't believe any of this." She looked at her husband. "Did you find out what happened back then?"

Perry nodded. "Bill told me this morning. Wendy and her friends were going to make Halloween costumes and they ran into Cindy at the fabric store. Cindy was there buying fabric to make real clothes. They made fun of her for it, but Cindy threw the last insult at Wendy, something about her hair. Anyway, Wendy stole some shears from the store and followed Cindy with the idea of cutting *her* hair and teaching her a lesson. Cindy's walk home went through the woods and that's where Wendy jumped her. They fought, things got out of hand and the shears ended up in Cindy's neck."

I remembered Rusty Melman had told me they knew a wound to the neck had killed Cindy. "Melman said the jugular had been severed. Probably bled out before Wendy could even think about getting help."

Perry nodded. "She panicked, remembered the story about the moose and how it had looked and started carving up the body."

"*Perry*," Della said and pushed her plate to the center of the table. "That's awful. I can't even imagine."

We were silent for a moment, either not sure how upset Della was or imagining a teenage girl carving up the body of another teenage girl. I caught Perry staring at me. "What?"

"You told me it was Vick Tomlinson."

"I thought it was. This all came about from me seeing him in the car with the Idaho license plates, remember? I talked to Vick this morning at the ceremony. He's a long distance cyclist. He rode his bike here from Eugene. Can you believe that? Turns out they were both staying at the Blue Bucket Inn and he borrowed Corsmo's car to buy supplies for his return trip and got a flat." Perry nodded like he understood the whole thing. "You look like that makes sense to you," I said. "A cross-state bike ride to play chess?"

"Sure," he said. "This is Oregon; people do that sort of thing. You'll see the signs on the highways for the bicycle routes. Don't people in Washington ride bikes?"

Carla and I shrugged and she glanced around the table. "So...can someone please tell me what happened to Ray's cell phone?"

Perry and I looked at each other across the table. "Go ahead," I told him.

He sighed. "This is the seventh anniversary of the Cedar Lake Chess Tournament. For those first six years an unfortunate tradition started where the winner of the tournament was taken outside and thrown into the lake. I know what you're thinking, but it was all in good fun. Until last year. Last year we had a winner who, like Ray, had never played in the tournament before and was unaware of the tradition and...he didn't know how to swim."

"Oh my," Carla said.

"Exactly," Perry said. "He was alright but I told everyone then that tossing the winner in the lake was done, never to happen again." He rubbed his forehead. "So this year — without my knowledge — a couple of guys got a big bucket of lake water, hid it inside and then dumped it on Ray when he won."

Carla laughed. "Why?"

Perry shrugged. "You know, like the football players who dump the Gatorade on their coach at the end of a game they win. Just having fun."

"They soaked my phone, the scoresheets, the board and pieces," I said. "It kind of pissed me off at first, but then it felt kind of good after the stress of the game."

Carla shook her head. "Chess players!"

"Hey," Perry said and looked at me, "you won the first Cedar Lake Chess Tournament you ever entered, and on top of that, you're the first one to win it undefeated." He raised his glass and said, "To my friend Ray Gordon, Cedar Lake Chess Champion!"

The thought of driving to Seattle with Morphy's body in the back of the car was a nauseating iciness. I couldn't let a strange vet take care of him either. He was my friend and I wouldn't abandon him in life or death.

We buried Morphy at the base of a big fir tree within sight of cabin six. He'd been so good in not getting caught I thought he should enjoy his stealthy skills for eternity. Jake and Wendy weren't there to object and Perry promised to keep it secret.

Perry had also graciously had someone clean the blood out of the Land Cruiser, though I had every intention of selling it as soon as possible. I just couldn't keep the car Morphy had died in, albeit as a hero, and Carla almost did. Maybe we would visit Mitch McCreedy again at Zephyr Auto Sales on the way out of town.

We packed our bags into the back and as Carla laid my trophy on the top she turned and said, "You won the chess tournament and caught two killers. Not a bad week, huh?"

"Not bad, but we lost Morphy."

She nodded and gave me a hug. "I'm sorry."

"Me too. He knew what he was doing though. That was only the second time in his life he'd attacked someone and both times it was to protect the family he loved."

"Oh, Ray. I wasn't his family."

"Oh yes you were. He knew you and I were *a we*."

"You think so?"

"Don't you?" I smiled. "Because I do."

We climbed into the car and she draped Morphy's collar over the rear view mirror. She tapped his ID tags so they jingled. "Let's go home."

ACKNOWLEDGEMENTS

While Jasper is based on an actual small town in Oregon, I decided to fictionalize it for the sake of the story as well as to preserve the originality and quality of the real thing. I won't mention the town here, but if you've been there then you know, and if you haven't but figure it out, do yourself a favor and visit.

A believable story often depends on small details and having friends with interesting occupations is a great help. Thank you to my friend and explosives expert, John Winn, for figuring out how much dynamite it takes to blow up a moose without disintegrating it.

The Mate in 2 chess problem from Chapter 21 was created by C. Mansfield in 1917. One solution, depending on the move black might make, is:

1. Be4, Nd2+
2. Nc4++

Also, thank you to all of my family, friends and readers who enjoy and support my books. Thank you so much.

The game Ray Gordon plays against Cal Pederson in Chapter 9 is an actual game played between Izhak Aloni and Bobby Fischer in 1968. I found this wonderful game in *Bobby Fisher's Outrageous Chess Moves: A Study of 101 Outrageous Moves by the Greatest Chess Champion of All Time* by Bruce Pandolfini (Fireside, 1993). The entire game between Aloni and Fischer is as follows:

Izhak Aloni vs Bobby Fischer
Vinkovci, Yugoslavia, 1968

WHITE	BLACK	WHITE	BLACK
1. d4	Nf6	23. Bxd6	Qe3+
2. c4	e6	24. Qxe3	dxe3
3. Nc3	Bb4	25. Re1	Bxc4
4. e3	b6	26. Rxe3	Bxa2
5. Bd3	Bb7	27. e5	Be6
6. Nf3	Ne4	28. Re1	Nb3
7. Qc2	f5	29. Ba6	Nc5
8. O-O	Bxc3	30. Be2	a5
9. bxc3	O-O	31. Bc7	a4
10. Nd2	Qh4	32. Bxb6	Nb3
11. f3	Nxd2	33. Bd1	Rc8
12. Bxd2	Nc6	34. Kf2	Nc1
13. Rae1	Na5	35. Re3	Rb8
14. Rb1	d6	36. Bc5	Rb2+
15. Be1	Qg5	37. Kg3	Nb3
16. Qe2	e5	38. Bd6	Nd4
17. e4	fxe4	39. Bg4	Bxg4
18. fxe4	Rxf1+	40. Kxg4	Rxg2+
19. Kxf1	c5	41. Kh3	Rg1
20. Kg1	Ba6	42. e6	Nf5
21. Bg3	cxd4	43. Rd3	g5
22. cxd4	exd4	44. Bg3	h5
		(0-1)	

Ray Gordon vs. Vick Tomlinson in Chapter 24 is an old tactical gem, Paul Morphy vs. Duke of Braunschweig and Count Isouard in 1858! I borrowed this game from *Winning Chess Tactics* (Microsoft Press, 1995) by International Grandmaster Yasser Seirawan with Jeremy Silman. As I reworded and paraphrased the expert analysis of that book for this novel, any mistakes or miscalculations are purely my own. The entire game of Paul Morphy vs. Duke of Braunschweig and Count Isouard is as follows:

Paul Morphy vs Duke of Braunschweig & Count Isouard
Paris, France, 1858

WHITE	BLACK
1. e4	e5
2. Nf3	d6
3. d4	Bg4
4. dxe5	Bxf3
5. Qxf3	dxe5
6. Bc4	Nf6
7. Qb3	Qe7
8. Nc3	c6
9. Bg5	b5
10. Nxb5	cxb5
11. Bxb5+	Nbd7
12. O-O-O	Rd8
13. Rxd7	Rxd7
14. Rd1	Qe6
15. Bxd7+	Nxd7
16. Qb8+	Nxb8
17. Rd8++	

The final match in the Cedar Lake Chess Tournament is another real game, in fact, Game 10 in the Australasian Championship from 1952 between Cecil Purdy and Ortvin Sarapu. This game is borrowed from the book, *The Search for Chess Perfection II* (Thinkers' Press, 2006) by CJS Purdy with John Hammond & Robert Jamieson. Again, any mistakes or miscalculations are purely my own. The entire game between Purdy and Sarapu is as follows:

Cecil J.S. Purdy vs Ortvin Sarapu
10th Game of the Australasian Championship, 1952

WHITE	BLACK	WHITE	BLACK
1. e4	e6	23. Qg5	Rf7
2. d4	d5	24. Nxf4	Rf5
3. Nc3	Bb4	25. Qg3	Bf7
4. e5	c5	26. h3	Qb3
5. a3	Bxc3+	27. Qe3	g5
6. bxc3	Qc7	28. Ne2	Bg6
7. Qg4	f5	29. g4	Rf7
8. Qg3	cxd4	30. Qxg5	Rg7
9. cxd4	Ne7	31. Qf6	Rf8
10. c3	O-O	32. Qxe6+	Bf7
11. a4	Nbc6	33. Qh6	Rg6
12. Nh3	Ng6	34. Qe3	Qc4
13. Be2	f4	35. Ng3	Be6
14. Qd3	Bd7	36. Nh5	Qc8
15. O-O	Rac8	37. f3	Qd8
16. Ba3	Nce7	38. Nf6+	Rfxf6
17. Bh5	Rf7	39. exf6	Qxf6
18. Rfc1	Qc4	40. Ra2	Qh4
19. Qb1	b6	41. Kg2	Rh6
20. Bxe7	Rxe7	42. Rh1	Resigns
21. Bxg6	hxg6		
22. Qxg6	Be8		

Made in the USA
Middletown, DE
16 April 2018